Dante's Paradise: A Retelling in Prose

David Bruce

Published by David Bruce, 2022.

This is a work of fiction. Similarities to real people, places, or events are entirely coincidental.

DANTE'S PARADISE: A RETELLING IN PROSE

First edition. July 5, 2022.

Copyright © 2022 David Bruce.

ISBN: 979-8201789688

Written by David Bruce.

Table of Contents

Dedication

Dedicated to Carl Eugene Bruce and Josephine Saturday Bruce

My father, Carl Eugene Bruce, died on 24 October 2013. He used to work for Ohio Power, and at one time, his job was to shut off the electricity of people who had not paid their bills. He sometimes would find a home with an impoverished mother and some children. Instead of shutting off their electricity, he would tell the mother that she needed to pay her bill or soon her electricity would be shut off. He would write on a form that no one was home when he stopped by because if no one was home he did not have to shut off their electricity.

The best good deed that anyone ever did for my father occurred after a storm that knocked down many power lines. He and other linemen worked long hours and got wet and cold. Their feet were freezing because water got into their boots and soaked their socks. Fortunately, a kind woman gave my father and the other linemen dry socks to wear.

My mother, Josephine Saturday Bruce, died on 14 June 2003. She used to work at a store that sold clothing. One day, an impoverished mother with a baby clothed in rags walked into the store and started shoplifting in an interesting way: The mother took the rags off her baby and dressed the infant in new clothing. My mother knew that this mother could not afford to buy the clothing, but she helped the mother dress her baby and then she watched as the mother walked out of the store without paying.

***

The doing of good deeds is important. As a free person, you can choose to live your life as a good person or as a bad person. To be a good person, do good deeds. To be a bad person, do bad deeds. If you do good deeds, you will become good. If you do bad deeds, you will become bad. To become the person you want to be, act as if you already are that kind of person. Each of us chooses what kind of person we will become. To become a good person, do the things a good person does. To become a bad person, do the things a bad person does. The opportunity to take action to become the kind of person you want to be is yours.

Human beings have free will. According to the Babylonian Niddah 16b, whenever a baby is to be conceived, the Lailah (angel in charge of contraception) takes the drop of semen that will result in the conception and asks God, "Sovereign of the Universe, what is going to be the fate of this drop? Will it develop into a robust or into a weak person? An intelligent or a stupid person? A wealthy or a poor person?" The Lailah asks all these questions, but it does not ask, "Will it develop into a righteous or a wicked person?" The answer to that question lies in the decisions to be freely made by the human being that is the result of the conception.

A Buddhist monk visiting a class wrote this on the chalkboard: "EVERYONE WANTS TO SAVE THE WORLD, BUT NO ONE WANTS TO HELP MOM DO THE DISHES." The students laughed, but the monk then said, "Statistically, it's highly unlikely that any of you will ever have the opportunity to run into a burning orphanage and rescue an infant. But, in the smallest gesture of kindness — a warm smile, holding the door for the person behind you, shoveling the driveway of the elderly person next door — you have committed an act of immeasurable profundity, because to each of us, our life is our universe."

In her book titled *I Have Chosen to Stay and Fight*, comedian Margaret Cho writes, "I believe that we get complimentary snack-size portions of the afterlife, and we all receive them in a different way." For Ms. Cho, many of her snack-size portions of the afterlife come in hip hop music. Other people get different snack-size portions of the afterlife, and we all must be on the lookout for them when they come our way. And perhaps doing good deeds and experiencing good deeds are snack-size portions of the afterlife.

• The Zen master Gisan was taking a bath. The water was too hot, so he asked a student to add some cold water to the bath. The student brought a bucket of cold water, added some cold water to the bath, and then threw the rest of the water on a rocky path. Gisan scolded the student: "Everything can be used. Why did you waste the rest of the water by pouring it on the path? There are some plants nearby which could have used the water. What right do you have to waste even a drop of water?" The student became enlightened and changed his name to Tekisui, which means "Drop of Water."

***

Educate Yourself
Read Like A Wolf Eats
Be Excellent to Each Other
Books Then, Books Now, Books Forever

***

In this retelling, as in all my retellings, I have tried to make the work of literature accessible to modern readers who may lack some of the knowledge about mythology, religion, and history that the literary work's contemporary audience had.

Do you know a language other than English? If you do, I give you permission to translate this book, copyright your translation, publish or self-publish it, and keep all the royalties for yourself. (Do give me credit, of course, for the original retelling.)

I would like to see my retellings of classic literature used in schools, so I give permission to the country of Finland (and all other countries) to give copies of any or all of my retellings to all students forever. I also give permission to the state of Texas (and all other states) to give copies of any or all of my retellings to all students forever. I also give permission to all teachers to give copies of any or all of my retellings to all students forever. Of course, libraries are welcome to use my eBooks for free.

Teachers need not actually teach my retellings. Teachers are welcome to give students copies of my eBooks as background material. For example, if they are teaching Homer's *Iliad* and *Odyssey*, teachers are welcome to give students copies of my *Virgil's* Aeneid: *A Retelling in Prose* and tell them, "Here's another ancient epic you may want to read in your spare time."

DEDICATED TO ROBERT WIEMAN

Fighting McCarthyism: Ohio University prof, Supreme Court, defeat loyalty oath

By David Bruce

Published 11 December 1989 in *The Athens News* (Ohio).

In 1950, Joe McCarthy, the junior senator from Wisconsin made a speech in Wheeling, West Virginia, that made him nationally prominent.

"Ladies and gentlemen, while I cannot take the time to name all the men in the State Department who have been named as active members of the Communist Party and members of a spy ring, I have here in my hand a list of 205—a list of names that were made known to the Secretary of State as being members of the Communist Party and who nevertheless are still working and shaping policy in the State Department."

Following that speech came years—the early to mid-1950s—in which McCarthy cast aspersions—with little or no evidence—about men and women innocent of any wrongdoing. McCarthy nearly immobilized two presidents, and because of his fame and the fear in which he cast the country, few dared to oppose him.

Ohio University Philosophy Professor Robert Wieman was exposed to much of that anti-communist hysteria in the early 1950s when he taught at Oklahoma A & M College. In a 1989 interview with *The Athens NEWS*, Wieman, who has taught at OU since the mid-'50s, told how in 1951, the Oklahoma legislature passed an anti-communist law, requiring all local and state employees to take a loyalty oath. The oath swore that the individual 1) was loyal to the United States, 2) was not a Communist, and 3) would bear arms, if necessary, in case of attack upon the United States.

Feeling that the law as drafted was unconstitutional, Wieman (a Navy veteran from 1942-46 who served much of the time in waters off Africa) and six other state employees at Oklahoma A & M went to court to force a test of the law's constitutionality. Eventually, the case which became known as Wieman vs. Updegraff, reached the U.S. Supreme Court.

But first, the case went before Oklahoma District Judge W.A. Carlisle, who rebuked the seven Oklahoma A & M employees:

"The people of the United States today are facing a terrible danger. We've reached the point where we must separate the wheat from the chaff.

These people want all the other protections of the government but they say they wouldn't fight to defend this country if necessary. I say it's a travesty of justice. It's an outrage for people like that to draw public funds. If Washington were alive today, I wonder what he'd say about something like this. In my opinion, a man that wouldn't defend his country if necessary has no right to draw its money."

Carlisle ordered that the employees be fired and their pay withheld. Eventually, though, the Supreme Court ruled in favor of Wieman and the other state employees. The front-page headline in *The New York Times* read, "Oklahoma's Oath of Loyalty Killed."

In the Supreme Court decision, issued Dec. 15, 1952, Justice Hugo Black wrote:

"The Oklahoma statute is but one manifestation of a national network of laws aimed at coercing and controlling the minds of men. Test oaths are notorious tools of tyranny. When used to shackle the mind they are, or at least they should be, unspeakably odious to a people. Governments need and have ample power to punish treasonable acts. But it does not follow that they must have power to punish thought and speech as distinguished from acts."

This case had two important ramifications, Wieman pointed out. First, he said, there was an "emphatic reaffirmation of the legal system." According to Wieman, "McCarthyism is almost any passionately fanatic movement. Whether the people are always sincere in using it or are using it as a vehicle to win elections doesn't matter." In a movement that is passionate and fanatic and perhaps even sincere, he pointed out, there is a tendency to "say that procedure doesn't matter, only the end matters."

During the McCarthy era, Wieman recalled, many people were "hesitant to defend the procedural safeguards for the modification of policy and the bringing of consensus among people." His case allowed the U.S. Supreme Court and later the Oklahoma Supreme Court to offer their prestige and eloquent statements about why these procedural safeguards are important, the OU professor said. The case reaffirmed that the American system of laws is a procedural system which should not be sacrificed for a passionate commitment to some end which fanatics believe outweighs other people's rights, he said.

In addition, Wieman maintained, accommodation—finding a way in which people can live together with the least mutual obstruction and the most mutual contribution—is one way for people and nations to live among one another. The Supreme Court case led to more accommodation, while it generated more opposition to McCarthyism.

Before that, however, through smear campaigns and negative campaigns, McCarthy won elections, "If you can win elections by this kind of thing, it becomes a feeding frenzy," Wieman said. "It's hard for people to express themselves effectively if [their opinion] isn't swimming with that tide."

Today [December 1989] Wieman sees a return of some of the characteristics of McCarthyism. Professionals are acknowledging that elections are won these days by politicians and their advisers doing whatever it takes to win, fair or foul.

This Wieman calls an "extremism in relation to the past." Until recently, he said, "although running for re-election was a major concern of people in office, they didn't spend all their term running for their next election.

"Most people, unless they were desperately out and unlikely to win without some wild extremism, were unlikely to commit themselves to things, in order to win an election, that would then interfere with their being able to meet the problems of the nation once in office," he said.

Today, Wieman said, there is a "curious combination of cynicism with a quite sincere factional suspicion of people who hold views different from what we do." For example, he pointed out, for the most part anti-abortion and abortion rights advocates are not seeking an accommodation with one another. It is much the same with other major issues, he said.

Also, in politics today there is the belief that any proposal, to meet a crisis, that costs money is not politically practical. "And so," Wieman said, "we have the oddity of national governors who will discuss needs and discuss possible solutions to those needs and will declare in favor of those solutions to those needs, but then assume that somebody else will have to fund it—state or local governments."

"Well, if you decide that someone else is going to do something and pay for it, that's not the way things are going to get done," he said. "They get done by the people who are going to pay for them deciding that's what should be done."

After a candidate is elected, the professor noted, he or she doesn't face the needs of the nation; instead the candidate thinks about "what did I say I was going to do and how can I squirm out of it if at all.

"It paralyzes government," just as McCarthyism paralyzed government in the early '50s, Wieman said.

When you have a win-at-any-costs political mentality, "courage [becomes] a terribly expensive thing to have," Wieman said. "You don't win by being courageous, you win by attacking from the outside; and if you are in, by being defensive, by rhetoric.

"Do anything and you make some enemies somewhere," he continued. "You can't do anything without influencing some people more favorably and other people less favorably, and so they're not going to regard you as their best friends anymore." Because of this, some politicians conclude that they ought not to do anything, he lamented.

A philosopher, Wieman explained that "in philosophy, we think we're engaged in inquiry, working out a commitment to the underlying principles of inquiry and the intellectual life." And so the philosopher doesn't regard teaching at a university as a job, in which the employee must leave all important decisions to higher-ups. After all, according to Wieman, "Universities are made up of people like philosophers; they're not made up by the chairman of the board of regents who hires somebody to stand in front of the class."

****

Robert Wieman (1920-2002)
 https://www.findagrave.com/memorial/123156906/
robert-m-wieman
 https://supreme.justia.com/cases/federal/us/344/183/

****

Now retired, David Bruce taught English and Philosophy at OU, and he wrote over 1,000 Wise Up! columns for *The Athens News.*

Note: Two characters in this book are Dante the Pilgrim and Dante the Poet. Dante the Pilgrim is the character who is going from Sphere to Sphere. Dante the Poet is the same character, but older and wiser. Dante the Poet has visited the Inferno, Purgatory, and Paradise and has much more knowledge than Dante the Pilgrim until the very end of the *Paradise*.

Chapter 1: Beatrice and Dante Rise from Eden

Dante the Poet thought, *God both created all things and keeps all things in existence as long as they exist. In each moment, God is engaged in the act of creation. If God were to stop His act of creation, all of the universe, including space and time, would go out of existence. God's glory is seen in the entire universe. In some places His glory can be seen more clearly. In some places His glory can be seen less clearly. Merit determines whether God's glory is seen more clearly or less clearly in human beings.*

I have traveled through the depths of the Inferno, I have climbed the Mountain of Purgatory, and I have risen from the Forest of Eden up through the cosmos and past it to the Mystic Empyrean, aka Paradise, the dwelling place of God. I have seen things that no person, once returned to Earth from Paradise, can tell about. Our goal is God, but after one experiences God and then returns to the mundane world, memory is powerless. Very little of the experience of God can be remembered and recounted. In Paradise, saved souls and Angels experience God continually.

What I can remember of my experience, I will recount in this, my work of art, my Paradise.

To do so, I need help. Apollo, ancient god of prophecy, please give me gifts enough to create a work of art that is worthy of a laurel crown. Previously, I have asked the Muses for their aid. I do so again, now, but I need your help as well because of the enormity and the difficulty of my task. Parnassus, the mountain of creative endeavor, has two peaks. One is dedicated to the nine Muses; the other is dedicated to you, Apollo. I ask for help in creation from all nine Muses and from you, Apollo.

Apollo, inspire me with the talent and the genius that you used to defeat Marsyas, the satyr who discovered a flute that played well by itself, without the help of living beings. Minerva had owned the flute, but she disliked the way her face contorted when she played it, and so she had discarded it. Marsyas found the flute, discovered the beauty of the sounds it made, and challenged you to a contest to see who made the best music. You defeated Marsyas. Please give me the use of the artistic gifts with which you defeated Marsyas.

Allow me to at least write the shadow of my experience of Paradise. If I can do even that, I will deserve the laurel crown that is given to persons who do great things. My lofty theme and your artistic inspiration will make me deserving of the laurel crown. Seldom are laurel leaves plucked to form a crown for politicians or for creators of works of art. Some forms of ambition are worthwhile, but are little pursued. When someone works hard to pursue such a crown, you, Apollo, should rejoice. Even if I fail in my pursuit, perhaps I may blaze the way for one who will succeed.

Now was the time of the spring equinox, a propitious time. The time was evening in the Forest of Eden.

Beatrice looked at the setting Sun. In the world of those who are still mortal, a person who did that would be blinded, but Beatrice was able to look at the Sun without harm, just as an eagle is alleged to be capable of doing. A ray of light directed straight at a mirror bounces back to its source. A pilgrim yearns to return to his or her spiritual home. Inspired by Beatrice, Dante the Pilgrim looked straight at the Sun as no one can in the Land of the Living.

In the Forest of Eden, saved souls can experience more than living souls can. Although Dante could not look at the Sun for very long, he did see sparks of light around the Sun. They looked like the sparks that appear when molten iron is poured. Later, in the Mystic Empyrean, Dante would again see sparks.

Suddenly, the light became much brighter, as if two Suns were shining. Beatrice continued to look at the Sun, and now Dante the Pilgrim looked at her eyes.

Beatrice thought, *Dante, you do not know it yet, but you have started to rise. Your soul has been purified. It is lighter than air, and naturally it rises through the air. From the Forest of Eden you have risen through the Sphere of Air and are passing through the Sphere of Fire. Dante, you lived in medieval times, and what you will experience is reality, but it is reality as a medieval person would expect to experience it. God wants to save your soul, and He will use what He needs to, to save it. God is willing for me to appear to you and be your guide through the cosmos until you reach God's dwelling place. Because you are a medieval person, God is willing for you to experience the cosmos as a medieval person would expect to experience it. As a medieval person, you believe that the Earth is the center of the universe. Around the Earth are first a Sphere of Air and then a Sphere of Fire, from which you believe lightning strikes the Earth. Then is the Sphere of the Moon. Although scientists will discover later that the Earth is not the center of the universe, God will let you experience the cosmos in the way that you expect it to be.*

God is willing to approach people through what they know or think they know. The lessons you will learn, of course, are eternal and unchanging and apply to your age as well as to much more modern ages.

As Dante the Pilgrim looked at Beatrice, he felt himself changing. The change was new, and he had never experienced it before. To describe it, he needed a new word: He was transhumanized. But such an experience of change cannot be described with a word or words. All he could do was to use as an analogy Glaucus, an ancient fisherman who noticed that fish revived when they were placed on a certain herb. Glaucus ate some of the herb, and he transformed into a sea-god and dived into the sea and experienced it as no human being has ever experienced it. Dante had changed, he had become more than human, and now he was rising to the heights of the cosmos.

Dante had changed, and he did not know that he was rising to the heights of the cosmos. Was he a soul only? Or was he a soul and a body? He did not know.

Dante had risen to the Sphere of Fire and was experiencing much light. Here he heard music: the music of the Spheres. As a medieval person, Dante believed that the boundary of the material universe was the Primum Mobile, something that a modern person might call outer space beyond the stars. In the medieval view of the cosmos, the Primum Mobile moved and imparted movement to the other Spheres of the cosmos, and that movement caused the music of the Spheres, something that living human beings normally do not hear.

Dante still did not know that he was rising. He was eager to learn the source of the music and the source of the light. Beatrice, like Virgil previously, knew Dante's thoughts. Beatrice was a good educator, and she started to answer his questions even before he voiced them.

Beatrice said, "You are not aware of the truth because you are not thinking correctly. You think that you are still in the Forest of Eden. You are not. You are rising. You have passed through the Sphere of Air and are now passing through the Sphere of Fire. You are moving quicker than lightning ever did."

Dante was pleased by what he had learned, but he now had a question: "How can I rise through these Spheres? How is that possible?"

Beatrice sighed. Dante did not have the knowledge that saved souls in Paradise have. She looked at Dante the way that a pitying mother looks at an ill child and said, "The universe has order, and that order is created by God and God's influence appears and can be seen throughout the universe. God created higher creatures — those with reason and the ability to experience love. These higher creatures include the Angels, human beings living on Earth, and the saved souls now with God in Paradise. Humanity has Paradise as the main goal. However, all created things, and not just the higher creatures, have a proper position in the cosmos.

"Some Spheres can be regarded as closer to God than others. The Inferno is as far away from God as it is possible to be. Things end up where they belong; they are attracted to their particular place — a place that reveals their relationship to God. This applies to Humankind as well. God wants each person to be saved and to rise. You and I have been purified, and being purified, we rise to our proper position in the cosmos.

"But not every person will be saved. God is a perfect Artist and a perfect Creator, but people have free will. Even though every person has as his or her goal Paradise, a person can go astray and pick up sin that weighs down that person's soul and makes it impossible to rise. Without repentance, one's soul can be so heavy that it is able only to fall into the Inferno.

"You should not be surprised that, having repented and purged your sins, you are rising. Your rising now is as natural as water flowing down a mountain. You should be surprised only if, having repented and purged your sins, you had not risen."

Beatrice then turned her gaze upward.

Chapter 2: Moon — Dark Spots

Dante the Poet thought, *Pay attention, readers. You have journeyed with me through the Inferno and up the Mountain of Purgatory, but the journey to Paradise is much more difficult. Think about whether you will be able to make the journey. This is a journey for a ship, not for a small boat. All who will follow in my wake should have a substantial vessel and should follow me closely for their own safety. The way to Paradise is a difficult one. For me to describe that way, I need the help of Apollo and the nine Muses, and I need Minerva — the goddess of wisdom — to fill my sails. If you have long sought the bread of Angels — the knowledge of God — then you may follow my ship in its journey, but you will be amazed by what you learn. You will be more amazed than the Argonauts who sailed with Jason in search of the Golden Fleece, who saw Jason plow a field with two fire-breathing bulls, who saw Jason plant in the plowed field dragon's teeth, and who saw the dragon's teeth grow into armed soldiers.*

Dante the Pilgrim and Beatrice rose into the heavens as fast as human eyes can rise to look at the sky. Dante looked at Beatrice, and Beatrice looked into the heavens. And as quickly as an arrow strikes its target after flying through the air after having been released by an archer, Dante and Beatrice reached the Moon. Beatrice told Dante, "Think of God and thank him, for He has raised us to the Sphere of the Moon."

Dante saw what seemed to be a milky cloud, and Beatrice and he were *inside* the Moon. Dante wondered how that could be. How can a solid be admitted into another solid and both remain intact just like light can enter water and the water remains intact? If Dante still had his body, which he was not sure he had, his being inside the Moon with an intact body was more than remarkable. He wanted to see something else more than remarkable: Jesus, in Whose human body divinity was infused without lessening either the human nature or the divine nature of His being. Once saved souls are in the Mystic Empyrean, they will understand things that reason cannot comprehend. Things that reason cannot comprehend in the Land of the Living will appear self-evident in the Mystic Empyrean.

Dante said to Beatrice, "I am grateful to God who has raised me from the Forest of Eden to the Moon. Please tell me something: What are the dark spots of the Moon? People tell stories about them on Earth. They say that God took Cain and placed him on the Moon and made him carry a bundle of thorns on his back, and they say that the dark spots of the Moon are really Cain and his bundle of thorns."

Amused, Beatrice smiled and said, "Human judgment often goes wrong, especially when no one can be present and see what is being speculated about. This should be no surprise, After all, when someone is present and can use the sense of sight and the other senses, errors can still be made. Optical illusions, mirages, hallucinations, and simple errors of judgment show this.

"Let me say that many of your ideas about the Moon are, quite simply, wrong, as will be shown with the rise of science in the future.

"You believe that the Moon both reflects the light of the Sun and has its own luminosity. Actually, the Moon does not have its own luminosity. It only reflects the light of the Sun.

"You believe that the Moon is smooth and without cracks. Actually, the Moon has mountains and craters and other geographical features. Any part of the Moon that is shadowed by mountains will be dark and will not reflect light. The Moon has different minerals. Some are shiny and reflect light well, and others are dark and absorb light instead of reflecting it. These things that I have mentioned explain the dark spots of the Moon.

"Of course, that is the scientific explanation, and the scientific explanation is a good one. If God had been incarnated in a later age, He could have said, 'Give to Caesar what is Caesar's, give to Einstein what is Einstein's, and give to God what is God's.' A man named Albert Einstein will be a famous scientist centuries from now.

"But we can give another explanation of the dark spots of the Moon. This explanation will be poetic and spiritual and is not meant to displace the scientific explanation. This explanation is simply another way of regarding the dark spots of the Moon to see what we may learn from them.

"People of your age — the medieval age — believe that the stars and the planets have an influence on human beings, who nevertheless have free will. Of course, a later age will discover that the stars and the planets have no influence on human beings. It is true that human beings are influenced by their heredity and environment, but they still have reason and free will that they can use to learn the right thing to do and then do it. Human beings are responsible for their actions and should not blame the stars and the planets for what they do.

"One way of looking at the dark spots of the Moon is that this is an example of God's mark on the universe. Listen to me carefully: God's glory is seen in the entire universe, which He created. The dark spots of the Moon are an illustration of this: In some places God's glory can be seen more clearly. In some places God's glory can be seen less clearly.

"God, by the way, will use what you know, or what you think you know, in order to teach you. You and other people of your time believe that the Earth is at the center of the universe and the Sun revolves around it. People of later ages will discover that the Earth revolves around the Sun, which is the center of our solar system. However, during our journey to the Mystic Empyrean, we will visit places in the cosmos in the order in which you would expect to visit them. In addition, when we visit planets, we will meet souls who have the qualities that people of your time associated with that particular planet.

"First, we are visiting the Moon, which is associated with faith. The Moon waxes and wanes, and throughout our lives our faith in God can also wax and wane. It can grow or diminish.

"Second, we will visit Mercury, which is associated with hope.

"Third, we will visit Venus, which is associated with love.

"Fourth, we will visit the Sun, which is associated with wisdom.

"Fifth, we will visit Mars, which is associated with courage.

"Sixth, we will visit Jupiter, which is associated with justice.

"Seventh, we will visit Saturn, which is associated with contemplation.

"Eighth, we will visit Gemini, a constellation of the Fixed Stars. The Fixed Stars are the constellations and other stars. The planets move around in the sky, but the stars of The Big Dipper, Gemini, and other constellations are always fixed in position relative to each other.

"Ninth, we will visit the Primum Mobile, which is the outermost moving Sphere. The Primum Mobile gives the planets and stars their motion.

"Finally, we will visit the Mystic Empyrean, which is the dwelling place of God. The Mystic Empyrean does not move, and it is outside space and time.

"You use the words 'star' and 'planet' interchangeably. You also call the Sun a planet. I will use the word 'planet' to refer to the Earth, the Moon, Mercury, Venus, Mars, Jupiter, and Saturn only.

"Souls will be at each place we visit so that you can talk to and learn from them.

"One of the things you will learn is this: Merit determines whether God's glory is seen more clearly or less clearly in human beings.

"God is intelligent, and His infinite intelligence is reflected in our finite intelligence. God is infinitely good, and His infinite goodness is reflected in our finite goodness.

"Each of us reflects God's glory differently. A morally good person reflects God's goodness well; a morally bad person reflects God's goodness badly."

Chapter 3: Moon — Piccarda and the Empress Constance (Unfulfillment of Religious Vows)

Dante was happy with what he had learned from Beatrice, and he raised his eyes, thinking to speak to her. But immediately he saw before him, vaguely, faces. The faces were indistinct; looking at each face was like looking at a pearl lying against pearly white skin.

Dante looked behind him, thinking that they were reflections. In doing so, he made a mistake that was the opposite of the mistake Narcissus had made. Narcissus had seen his own reflection in a pool of water, and he fell in love with it, mistaking a reflection for a real thing. Dante, however, mistook what is real for reflections. The faces really were in front of him, pale and indistinct as they were.

Beatrice saw Dante turn around. She smiled and said to him, "Don't be surprised at my smiling at your mistake. The evidence is in front of your eyes, but you do not believe it. You look in back of yourself although nothing is there to see. The faces you see in front of you really are in front of you. They are here because they broke their vows. They are here so that you may learn from them. Speak to them. Believe what they say. They are perfected souls who are blessed by God, and they will not mislead you."

Dante faced the souls, and to the soul who seemed most anxious to talk to him he said, "Soul, you who are well created and who enjoy Paradise and endless life, things whose goodness cannot be truly known until they are experienced, please tell me who you are and please tell me your fate."

The soul, happy, replied, "We are filled with love, as is our Creator, and we will happily respond to a just request such as the one that you have made.

"I was a nun: a virgin sister. Think, and remember, and you will find that you know me. You have not recognized me because I am more beautiful than I ever was on Earth. I am Piccarda."

Dante thought, *Indeed, I remember you, Piccarda. You are a member of the Donati family, whom I know well in Florence. Your brother is Forese Donati, who while alive exchanged comic insult poems with me. I recently saw Forese being purged of gluttony on ledge six of the Mountain of Purgatory. Cianfa Donati, another member of the Donati family, is among the thieves in the Inferno. Forese* told me that Corso, his brother, will end up in Hell. Obviously, your family does not get you into Heaven or Hell; your own freely willed actions do that.*

Piccarda continued, "I and the other souls appear here because we failed to keep our vows in some way. We promised something, and we did not do what we promised."

Dante thought, *You were a nun, Piccarda, but your evil brother, Corso, forced you to leave your religious order and get married. You made a vow as a nun, but because of Corso you could not keep your vow. You had entered a nunnery, but Corso, who is both a brute and your brother, forced you to leave the nunnery and make a political marriage — a marriage that politically benefited Corso.*

Beatrice thought, *Corso, Piccarda's brother, is the leader of the Black Guelfs in Florence, and he is the person who will persuade Pope Boniface VIII to send Charles of Valois and his troops to Florence — the military action that will lead to the exile of Dante from Florence. Corso will attempt to gain control of Florence, but he will fail. He will be captured, and when he tries to escape, he will take a spear to the throat and die. He will die on 6 October 1308.*

Piccarda continued, "I and the other souls you see are appearing here on the Moon, which is the slowest Sphere."

Beatrice thought, *The closer a Sphere is to the Earth, according to Dante's medieval beliefs, the slower it moves. The Moon is the closest to the Earth, and therefore it moves the slowest. The Primum Mobile is the furthest away from the Earth, and therefore it moves the fastest.*

Piccarda continued, "We are in the slowest Sphere, and we are happy to be here because this is where God put us. We are here because of our failure to keep our vows in some way."

Dante replied, "Your face is transformed. It glows and is brilliant and is more beautiful than it was on Earth. I did not recognize you until you spoke to me, but now I remember and know you. Please tell me something. All of you souls I see here are happy, and all of you souls are in the slowest and the lowest Sphere. Do any of you wish to be in a higher Sphere? Do any of you wish to be higher in Paradise?"

Piccarda and the other souls smiled, and Piccarda, as happy as a woman newly in love, said, "We want only what we have, nothing more. We want only what God gives us. Our desires are aligned with the will of God. If we wished to be higher in Paradise, then our desires would not be aligned with the will of God, and we would not be perfected souls.

"Think about love and what it is. To be here is to exist in Love. All who are in Paradise exist in Love. Our will and God's will are perfectly aligned, and we feel Perfect Love. All in Paradise are happy with whichever heavenly Sphere they are associated. We find our peace in the will of God. Everyone in Paradise is perfectly happy and blissful. All of us souls experience all the happiness that we are capable of experiencing."

Dante knew then that all of the Spheres reflect God's glory. He also knew that in some Spheres God's glory can be seen more clearly and in some Spheres God's glory can be seen less clearly. Dante also knew that no one needs to have a perfect life on Earth to be in Paradise later. If people would need to be perfect on Earth in order to be in Paradise later, Paradise would be empty. Nevertheless, Paradise is a meritocracy. To recognize that one has sinned and to sincerely repent one's sins are major accomplishments.

Dante asked Piccarda for more details about her unfulfilled vow.

Piccarda responded, "Saint Clare, the founder of the Franciscan Order of Poor Clares, inspired me to become a nun in her order. She had been a noblewoman of wealth and beauty, and in 1212, she and Saint Francis founded the first Franciscan convent for women. Saint Clare had great virtue, and she is in the Mystic Empyrean with God. I left mundane things to follow her, and I joined the Poor Clares. I resided in the convent, and I made a religious vow to be a nun for the rest of my life. But men, led by my brother Corso, all of whom understood hate more than they understood love, took me — by force — from the convent. Corso forced me to marry to seal a political alliance that would benefit him.

"This soul to my right also experiences the love of God, and she also experienced what I experienced on Earth. She, also, was a nun. She, also, was forced to leave the convent. She, also, was forced to marry. Even though she was forced to do all these things, she wore — in her heart — the habit of a nun. This soul on Earth was the Empress Constance. Her father-in-law was Frederick Barbarossa. Her son is the Holy Roman Emperor Frederick II. Her grandson is Manfred."

Dante thought, *Constance, of course, is in Paradise, but her son, the Holy Roman Emperor Frederick II, is in the Inferno with the other heretics. Constance's grandson, Manfred, is among the Late Repentant (in the group of the excommunicated) in AntePurgatory. Once again, we see that family does not determine where you end up in the afterlife. Also, we see an Empress side by side with a member of the Florentine middle class. In Paradise, royalty and commoners mix.*

Having finished speaking, Piccarda sang "*Ave Maria*":
"Hail, Mary,
"Full of grace,
"The Lord is with you.
"Blessed are you
"And blessed
"Is the fruit of your womb.
"Holy Mary,
"Mother of God,
"Pray for us
"Sinners
"Now and in
"The hour of our death."
Singing, she disappeared as if sinking into deep water.
Dante turned to Beatrice, but she was shining so brightly that he could not look at her, and so he found it difficult to ask her questions.

Chapter 4: Moon — Location of Souls (The Absolute Versus the Conditional Will)

Dante had two questions that he wished — equally — to ask Beatrice. He was like a man who stood exactly in between two equally delicious meals — he would starve to death before choosing which to eat. He was like a lamb that stood exactly between two equally menacing wolves. He was like a dog that stood exactly in between two equally enticing does.

Unable to choose which question to ask first, Dante stood without speaking, but his face showed his desire to speak.

Beatrice then did what Daniel did. King Nebuchadnezzar had a dream that he wanted his advisers to recount and to interpret. His advisers were unable to do these things and so he ordered that they be executed. But Daniel was able to recount and to interpret the dream, thus appeasing Nebuchadnezzar. Beatrice appeased Dante.

Beatrice said to Dante, "I see that you desire to ask two questions, and that you are unable to speak. Your first question is this: 'If my will remains good, how can another person's forcing me to act against my will mean that I receive less of a reward?' You also want to ask, 'Where do the souls of the saved go after death? Is it true that all souls return to their particular planet or star, as we read in Plato?'

"Those are the two questions you wish to ask. I will answer the second question first because the result will be very harmful if it is answered incorrectly.

"Where do the souls of the saved go after death? All of them go to the same place: Paradise, aka the Mystic Empyrean. This is where the Angels, including the highest order of the Angels, are. This is where Moses and Samuel are. This is where John the Baptist and John the Apostle are. This is where Mary, the Mother of Jesus, is. The souls you have seen here, and all of the other saved souls, do or will (if they are still climbing the Mountain of Purgatory or if their body is still alive) reside there. Each soul will have eternal bliss. Paradise is in the Mystic Empyrean, and it is where God resides.

"You have seen souls here on the Moon not because the Moon is where these souls stay, but simply because these souls are appearing before you in order to educate you. You will see souls on other planets and other places. Where they appear will reveal the greater or the lesser degree of their blessedness. The Moon is the lowest planet, and these souls are less blessed than other souls, although they are fully and eternally happy and reside in the same place as Mary.

"The souls are appearing before you in these places and in this way because this is a form of education from which your mind will be able to benefit. Your mind and the minds of other living human beings acquire knowledge through experience and the use of the senses, which give your minds information that your reason can consider.

"This is something that God is willing to do and has done. For example, sacred scripture mentions the hands and feet of God even though God, of course, is immaterial and has no hands and feet. For example, we use spatial terms to describe Paradise, which lies outside space and time — 'outside' is a spatial term that does not apply literally to Paradise. The Holy Church presents Archangels that have human features although Archangels are immaterial beings. All of these things are done to help Humankind understand.

"Plato in his *Timaeus* spoke about a myth in which souls exist on planets and stars, acquire material form and live on Earth, and then after death return to the planet or star from which they came. If this is meant to be taken literally, it is false. Souls are created by God and do not exist before the body.

"If Plato's myth is taken figuratively, then perhaps what is meant is that the planets and the stars have some influence on human life. Your age believed that, but science will later show that astrology is false. The Romans gave the planets names such as Jupiter and Mercury and Mars, but these names led the world astray.

"Still, one element of truth remains. Plato may be saying, figuratively, that after death the soul retains what made it distinctive and individual in the living world. You will still be you, even after death.

"The main point for you to learn here is that the dwelling place of Piccarda Donati and the Empress Constance is in the Mystic Empyrean with God. Their eternal dwelling place is not on the Moon. The souls in Paradise are helpful, and these souls made an appearance on the Moon to educate you about the degrees of blessedness in Paradise. Merit determines whether God's glory is seen more clearly or less clearly in human beings. In these souls who appeared to you on the Moon, God's glory is seen, but it is seen less clearly than in other souls.

"Your other question is this: 'If my will remains good, how can another person's forcing me to act against my will mean that I receive less of a reward?'

"This question arises from a misunderstanding of the will. Absolute will exists, and conditioned will exists. Absolute will is like a flame that always desires to rise although it can be forced to the side if something such as a stone is held directly above it.

"Conditioned will gives in, to some extent. Violence can force will to give in, and a conditioned will can continue to give in even after the violence has stopped.

"Such was the case with Piccarda and the Empress Constance. Evil men used violence to take them out of the convent. Piccarda and the Empress Constance cannot be blamed for that. But their will became conditioned, and after the violence ceased, they remained instead of running back to the convent to be nuns.

"Absolute will does not give in, even when faced with bad consequences. If the choice is to give in and remain married or to run back to the convent to keep a vow made to God to be a nun even though that can result in *being hunted down and murdered*, the absolute will chooses running back to the convent to be a nun.

"This is more than a theory. For example, Saint Lawrence, a deacon of the Church of Rome, was ordered to hand over the treasures of the Church. He gathered a group of ill and poor people and called them the treasures of the church although he knew, of course, that his tormentors wanted material treasures. His tormentors tortured him and grilled him alive. He told them that one side was done, so turn him over and eat. His absolute will refused to allow his will to be conditioned and give up the Church's material treasures — thereby violating his oath to protect the Church's treasures — although the alternative to allowing his will to be conditioned was a horrible death. Absolute will never consents to doing the wrong thing, no matter the consequences.

"Here's another example, Gaius Mucius attempted but failed to kill the Etruscan King Porsena. He was told that he could either give information about the Romans' defenses or be executed. Mucius put his right hand in a fire and allowed it to be burned off to show that he would not be a traitor to his country. Instead, he would be faithful to his vow to be loyal to his country.

King Porsena allowed Mucius to live. Thereafter, Mucius was known by the nickname '*Scaevola*' — 'Lefthanded.'

"Piccarda and the Empress Constance should have kept their vow. Saint Lawrence had vowed not to hand over the material treasures of the Church, and Scaevola had vowed loyalty to the Romans. Both kept their vows, despite the consequences. But such firm will as they showed is seldom seen.

"But here arises another question. Do what Piccarda said and what I said contradict each other? Piccarda said that the Empress Constance always wore the habit of a nun in her heart. Of course, the will of Empress Constance had become conditioned. Often, someone will consent to doing the wrong thing out of fear that something worse will occur.

"For example, Alcmeon did this. His father was Amphiaraus, a soothsayer who knew that he would die if he took part in a war against Thebes and so hid himself. Polynices, the leader of the forces against Thebes, bribed Eriphyle, the wife of Amphiaraus, with a gold necklace to reveal her husband's hiding place. Forced to go to war against Thebes, Amphiaraus asked Alcmeon to vow to avenge him, and Alcmeon killed his mother, Eriphyle. Alcmeon faced a choice: either kill his mother or risk being impious by disobeying his father. He did something evil because he was afraid that if he did not, he would do something even more evil.

"The Empress Constance did the same thing. She remained and stayed married and broke her vow although she could have run back to the convent and been a nun. She chose the lesser of what she considered to be two evils: being married, rather being killed. Absolute will would not have consented to this.

"When Piccarda spoke of the Empress Constance wearing the habit of a nun in her heart, she was referring to her absolute will. When I was speaking of the Empress Constance's actions, I was referring to her conditioned will. Piccarda and I did not contradict each other."

Dante understood. He said to Beatrice, "Thank you. All humans want to acquire truth, and acquiring truth is a process of asking questions and learning the answers until we are in Paradise and happy in our full knowledge. I understand the answers to the two questions that I had before, but now I have a third question: Is it possible to mend a broken vow to God by substituting good deeds for it?"

Beatrice looked at Dante. Her eyes sparkled with love, and Dante felt as if it he was about to faint. Beatrice had become more radiant.

13

Chapter 5: Moon — Compensation for Broken Vows

Beatrice said to Dante, "You see that I have become more radiant. You will continue to see this. My radiance comes from the joy I feel as I come closer to God and as I see others, such as you, come closer to God. I can see that in your mind Eternal Light shines. One who comes closer to God comes closer to the perfect sight that sees the Eternal Good.

"Sometimes, people pursue the wrong thing through a misunderstanding of the right thing. The right thing should be understood, and it should be pursued.

"You wish to know whether a broken vow to God can be fixed with a substitution such as good deeds for what was vowed. You wish to know whether such a substitution would be acceptable in the eyes of God.

"Be aware that the greatest gift that God has given Humankind is free will. This is a gift that is most like God. This is the gift that God most cherishes. God gifted only intelligent beings such as human beings and Angels with free will.

"When we make a religious vow, we are giving back to God that gift — we are sacrificing our freedom for God. It is wrong to take back that gift. We sacrifice free will when we make a vow. For example, we are free to make and keep as much money as we can. However, if we make a vow of voluntary poverty so that we can serve God better, we give up part of our free will — we are no longer free to make and keep as much money as we can.

"When we make a vow, God can either consent to it or not consent to it. If the vow is evil, God will not consent to it. But if the vow is good, God will consent to it, and it becomes binding.

"Because free will is your most precious possession, nothing can make up for it because nothing is as precious as it is. Nothing can compensate for the free will that the person making a religious vow to God has sacrificed. The person making a religious vow is giving God the greatest gift possible: the sacrifice of free will by substituting dedication to God for free will. Someone who breaks that kind of vow is taking back something that no longer belongs to him or her.

"However, the Church does grant dispensations for vows. Let me explain why and how. Pay attention. Be sure to retain this information.

"Vows consist of two parts. First is the act of promising, and second is what is promised. The act of promising cannot be annulled. However, what is promised can be changed in special circumstances.

"For example, Jews would make a vow to sacrifice to God. This is a vow that had to be kept, but the substance of the sacrifice could change. Instead of sacrificing one particular kind of crop, another kind of crop could be sacrificed.

"But whenever some substitution is made, it cannot be made simply by one's own choice. This is something that the Church must approve. Remember the gold and silver keys of Saint Peter.

"In addition, the substitution must be of greater value than what was originally promised. If someone vowed four, then got the approval of the Church to make a substitution, that person must pay six. A person may have vowed to volunteer a certain number of hours to a charity each year. Should that person fall into circumstances that make volunteering impossible, the Church may approve the donation of money as a substitute, but the value of the money to be donated must be more than the value of the volunteer hours that were vowed.

"In addition, be aware that some vows admit of no substitution. What can substitute for a vow of a lifetime of service?

"Therefore, Humankind must be careful to take vows seriously and not make vows rashly. Also, vows must be made rightly and ethically and must not result in evil. God does not accept all vows; God rejects those vows that result in evil.

"Remember the rash vow that Jephthah made. This King of Israel went off to fight the Ammonites. He vowed to God that if he were victorious that he would then sacrifice to God the first thing that he saw coming out of the door of his house when he returned from battle. The first thing that he saw coming of the door of his house was his daughter, and he sacrificed her. Jephthah's vow was blind and rash, and he did evil by keeping it. Far better would have been for him to say, 'My vow was wrong,' and not keep it. Such a vow is not the kind that God approves.

"Remember the rash vow that Agamemnon, the leader of the Greek forces against Troy, made. He vowed to sacrifice to Artemis the loveliest creature born in a certain year. That year saw the birth of his daughter Iphigenia, and she was the loveliest creature born that year. He did not sacrifice her then, but years later, when bad winds kept the Greek ships from sailing to Troy, other people blamed the bad winds on Agamemnon's failure to keep his vow. Agamemnon sacrificed his daughter, good winds began to blow, and the Greek ships sailed to Troy.

"When interpreting the worthiness of vows, or sacred scripture, remember that God is omnibenevolent. God always wishes good; God never wishes evil.

"Learn from the rash vows, Christians. Be wary of rushing to make vows. You need a good, weighty reason to make a vow. You need more than a feather in the wind. And don't think that making reparations for a broken vow is easy. It will take more than a few drops of holy water!

"You do not need to make vows to wash away your sins. You have the Old Testament and the New Testament, and you have the Church. With these, you can save your soul. I repeat: You do not need to make vows to be saved. You have the Bible and the Church; these are enough for you to be saved.

"Some people may try to sell you releases from your vows. This is a scam. Don't fall for it! Jews keep their vows although they lack the New Testament, and they will laugh at you if you fall for such scams although you have both the Old Testament and the New Testament and also the Church to guide you. Stick with the trusted guides and ignore the scammers."

Beatrice then looked upward, and she and Dante rose to the next Sphere: Mercury. Beatrice, now closer to God, glowed more brightly, and the planet reflected her brightness. Mercury is a planet that reacted to Beatrice's brightness. Dante, who has a soul and is coming closer to God, reacted more strongly to Beatrice's brightness.

The fish in a pond will investigate whatever is new, thinking it may be nourishing. Here on this planet, over a thousand souls came toward Dante and Beatrice, saying, "Behold another who will increase our love." Love in Paradise is something that increases the more it is shared.

Each of the souls shone with the brightness of love.

Dante the Poet thought, *If I were to stop writing here and not describe what happened next, you, Reader, would crave to know what happened. You would then understand how keen I was to learn from these souls.*

One of the souls said to Dante, "Blissful one, whom God allows to travel through Paradise although you are still alive, please ask us anything you want. The light of God shines in us as it shines throughout the Heavens."

Beatrice encouraged Dante to do as the soul asked: "Ask whatever you want to ask. These souls are helpful, and they are trustworthy."

Dante said to the soul, "You, saved soul, are bright with light. I do not know who you are, or why you are showing yourself to me on this planet that is often hidden from Humankind because it is so close to the Sun."

The saved soul heard Dante and then glowed with much more brightness than previously. The Sun usually glows so brightly that Humankind cannot look at it and see its mass; the saved soul was hidden from Dante because of the soul's brightness.

Chapter 6: Mercury — Roman Emperor Justinian

The saved soul spoke, "The story of the Roman Empire is the story of the Roman Eagle. The Eagle followed the course of Heaven. The Sun rises in the East and sets in the West, and Aeneas, the prince of conquered Troy, journeyed West to Italy, wed Lavinia, and became an important ancestor of the Roman people.

"Constantine, however, reversed that direction. He took the Eagle Eastward, from Rome to Constantinople. In doing so, he went against the course of Heaven — the Sun travels from East to West, and taking the Eagle to Constantinople reversed that course.

"For approximately 200 years, the Eagle remained in the East, close to Troy, and then my day came, and I and people under my command reconquered Italy for the Empire.

"I was a Roman Emperor; I am still Justinian. I, inspired by God, reformed the Roman law."

Beatrice thought, *The Roman Empire was huge, and in order to better manage it, it was divided into two centers of power. One was the Western Roman Empire, which people call the Roman Empire. Its center was at Rome. Eventually, Rome fell as Germanic tribes made war against the Western Roman Empire. However, the other Empire continued.*

The other Empire was the Eastern Roman Empire, which people call the Byzantine Empire. Its center of power was at the city named Byzantium. In Roman times, this city was known as Constantinople. Later, it will officially be known as Istanbul. The supremacy of the Eastern Roman Empire ended in 1204 C.E., when Constantinople was sacked in the Fourth Crusade.

Justinian (485-565 C.E.) was one of the Byzantine Emperors. Two centuries before, Constantine had moved to the Eastern Roman Empire, making his home in Constantinople, which of course was named after him.

Justinian is known as a lawgiver and Roman Emperor. His upbringing was humble. He was born a peasant, but he was adopted at age eight by his uncle Justin. Justin took him to Constantinople and renamed him Justinian. His original name was Petrus Sabbatius.

Justinian has a connection with Ravenna, Italy, where Dante will die. In Ravenna, Justinian ordered beautiful buildings to be created; they are decorated with mosaics. Dante will live in Ravenna at the end of his life. Justinian's general, Belisarius, was able to conquer Rome, thus making it part of the Empire again and allowing Justinian to create magnificent buildings in Ravenna.

Justinian's major Earthly accomplishment was having the Roman law codified — put in an orderly fashion. Before Justinian, Roman law was disorderly. Many Emperors had made many laws, and no one really knew what the law was, and so no one had any way of knowing what was legal and what was illegal. Justinian had people clean up the law — get rid of the old, outdated laws, and make sure that the current laws made sense. In addition, he had a commentary and a textbook of the law created — that way, people could study the law and so know what was legal and what was illegal.

One important effect of the Justinian Code is that people began to study it in the 12th century, as city-states and national monarchies developed in Europe. Dante studies the Justinian Code in Florence, and he believes that Italy needs a Roman Emperor to enforce the law. He feels that the Roman law of the Justinian Code is good.

Justinian continued, "Before I was able to accomplish this reform of Roman law, I needed to do other things. For example, I needed to get rid of a heresy that I believed. I believed that Jesus had only one nature. I believed that Jesus had only a divine nature. I should have believed that the incarnated Jesus is fully divine and fully human.

"Fortunately, Pope Agapetus the First was able to correct my heretical thinking. I trusted him. Pope Agapetus was a good spiritual leader, and he helped me to correct my thinking and to establish the right relationship between church and state. Pope Agapetus handled religious questions, while I handled legal, secular questions. And now that I am in Paradise, I can see clearly that Pope Agapetus got the answers to the religious questions right.

"You know that when two statements are contradictory, one statement must be true, and the other statement must be false. Both cannot be true. For example, only one of these statements is true: 1) A bachelor is an unmarried man. 2) A bachelor is not an unmarried man.

"As clearly as you know this kind of logic in the living world, so clearly do I know in Paradise that Jesus is both fully divine and fully human. What is a mystery in the living world is self-evident in Paradise.

"To be a great ruler, you have to get the answers to the ultimate questions right. If you are going to be a great ruler, you have to think correctly about God. Pope Agapetus helped me to think correctly about God. After I thought correctly about God, I was able to turn my attention to the reform of the Roman law.

"I also delegated authority. I let Belisarius be my general and fight my wars. He was such an able warrior and leader that I knew that God approved of such a delegation of duty. By allowing Belisarius to wage war when needed, I was able to focus on codifying the Roman law. Belisarius really was a good general. He was able to gain control of Italy, which had been overrun by Germanic tribes, and thus I was able to build beautiful buildings in Ravenna.

"By allowing Belisarius to handle war, I was able to devote myself to something that is more valuable: law. I wanted the world to be well governed. To do that, you need to have both the right faith and the right laws.

"I allowed people to do what they do best. The Pope was and is the authority in spiritual matters, and I did not challenge him for power. Belisarius was a very competent general, and I allowed him to lead the troops into battle. I myself was the right person to codify the Roman law, and I did that.

"This answers your first question: Who am I? But now I need to add something more. God supported the Roman Empire, and God wanted the seat of the Empire to be at Rome. Even now, a true Roman Emperor should exist.

"People do not support the Roman Empire nowadays. The Ghibellines have taken the imperial standard as their own, but they do not support the ideal of the Empire. The Guelfs support the French Emperor and try to suppress the imperial standard. Neither the Ghibellines nor the Guelfs deserve praise because neither group supports the ideal of the Empire — an ideal that God supports.

"Courage consecrated the Empire. Aeneas came to Italy, and he fought a war against those who would keep him from fulfilling his God-given destiny of becoming an important ancestor of the Roman people. When Aeneas went to Italy, Aeneas was shown around Latium, which was built on the future site of Rome. Pallas, whose father was Evander, the King of Latium, was old enough to go to war, and his father entrusted him to Aeneas. Unfortunately, Turnus, the leader of the forces arrayed against Aeneas, killed Pallas in battle. Aeneas avenged Pallas' death by killing Turnus.

"Aeneas established the imperial Eagle at Latium, but his son, Ascanius, moved the Eagle to Alba Longa, where it stayed for more than 300 years. By then, Rome had been built, and three heroes of Alba Longa fought three heroes of Rome to see which city would be superior. Two of the Roman heroes died, but the third Roman hero killed all three of the Alba Longan heroes, and the imperial Eagle went to Rome.

"The early Romans were mainly men, and they needed wives. They invited their neighbors, the Sabines, who would not allow their daughters to marry Roman men, to a festival, and when Romulus (the founder of Rome) gave a signal, the Romans fought off the Sabine men and kidnapped the young Sabine women. Romulus talked to the young Sabine women and convinced them to marry Roman men.

"Seven Kings ruled Rome over the years. Sextus Tarquinius, son of King Tarquinius Superbus, raped Lucretia, a Roman noblewoman, and as a result she committed suicide. Her brother led a rebellion that cast out King Tarquinius Superbus, the last King of the Romans. The Kingship was replaced by a republic, a kind of democracy in which leaders are elected by the people — or at least some of the people.

"The Romans fought often and won. The Eagle defeated Brennus, the leader of Gaul. The Eagle defeated Pyrrhus, the King of Epirus, who supported the Greeks.

"Titus Manlius Torquatus led the Romans to numerous victories. Lucius Quintius Cincinnatus was both a great general and a simple farmer. When the Romans ran into trouble, they requested that he leave his farm and lead the Roman soldiers against the enemy. After defeating the enemy, he retired again and worked on his farm.

"The Decii and the Fabii were prominent Roman families who produced many heroes and leaders.

"Scipio Africanus became a hero by defeating the great Carthaginian general Hannibal, who warred against Rome. When Hannibal first went to war against Rome, he achieved a notable feat: He brought war elephants to Italy by crossing the Alps from Spain into Italy. For years he roamed up and down Italy, but eventually Scipio Africanus defeated him in Africa. Again, the Eagle was triumphant.

"The story of Empire is part of your story. Catiline tried to take over political power, but the Roman orator Cicero stopped him. Catiline took refuge at Fiesole, a hill outside Florence, but he was defeated.

"All of us are a part of a much larger story. God has a plan for the world, and you are a part of that plan.

"Big events have consequences on the local level. A war of worldwide importance can definitely have an effect at the local level.

"Pompey fought Julius Caesar for power. Julius Caesar crossed the Rubicon River and fought many battles around the Mediterranean. Caesar finally defeated Pompey at the Battle of Pharsalia in 48 B.C.E., Pompey fled to Egypt, and Ptolemy killed him there.

"Julius Caesar defeated the rebels and invaders and gained all the power, but he was then assassinated by a number of Romans, including Brutus and Cassius, both of whom are punished in the deepest part of the deepest circle in the Inferno. Brutus and Cassius tried to stop God's plan for the Roman Empire. Following the assassination of Julius Caesar, many people suffered and died. Because of the action of Cassius and Brutus, civil war continued in Rome.

"Following the death of Julius Caesar, another power struggle broke out, this time between Octavian Caesar (the grand-nephew and adopted son of Julius Caesar) and Mark Antony. In 43 B.C.E., at Modena, Octavian defeated Mark Antony. In 41 B.C.E., at Perugia, Octavian defeated Lucius, Antony's brother.

"After Mark Antony and Octavian had worked together for a while, they began fighting each other. Mark Antony allied himself with Cleopatra, the Queen of Egypt. In 31 B.C.E., after Octavian defeated their forces at the Battle of Actium, a naval battle, Mark Antony and Cleopatra fled back to Egypt. Both of them committed suicide, Cleopatra by allowing a poisonous snake to bite her. Octavian became Caesar Augustus. He became the first Roman Emperor. With him, the Roman Republic ended. So did the civil wars.

"From roughly 27 B.C.E. to 180 C.E., Italy was at peace. Of course, fighting occurred on the edges of the Roman Empire, but Italy itself was at peace. This is known as the *Pax Romana*: the Roman Peace.

"Peace is a great blessing. Life during wartime is rough. Food is scarce to get. Women sell themselves to get enough to eat. Children starve. People kill and are killed.

"When Rome was at war, the doors of the temple of Janus were kept open. Because of Caesar Augustus, the doors were closed.

"Two especially important events occurred.

"First, during the reign of Tiberius, the third Caesar (that is, the second Roman Emperor; the first Caesar was Julius), Jesus Christ was crucified. This paid the price for the sin of Adam, and at the same time Christ's crucifixion was a new sin.

"Second, in 70 C.E., Titus conquered and destroyed Jerusalem. At the time, Titus' father, Vespasian, was the Roman Emperor. Later, Titus became Roman Emperor, serving from 79-81 C.E. The destruction of Jerusalem was just vengeance for the death of Christ.

"I began my history of the Roman Empire in the middle by telling about Constantine and myself. Then I went back in time to the beginnings. Now I will jump ahead in time to Charlemagne. From near the end of the first century, we are going 700 years ahead in time.

"Charlemagne defended the Church against a man he dethroned: King Desiderius, the Lombard. In a later age, Charlemagne is called the Holy Roman Emperor, but he called himself simply the Roman Emperor. He became Emperor in 800 C.E. Charlemagne's story is the continuing story of the Roman Empire.

"Now let's look at the present age: 1300 C.E. This is another big jump in time.

"The Guelfs and Ghibellines are in conflict in Florence. Both political parties are working against the Empire.

"The Guelfs are supporting the Pope against the Holy Roman Emperor. They are against the Empire. The Guelfs are allied with the French — symbolized by the yellow lilies.

"The Ghibellines want power for themselves. The Ghibellines say that they support the Holy Roman Emperor, but they are actually more concerned with getting power for themselves.

"What is needed is the formation of a competent world government. Neither the Guelfs nor the Ghibellines are helping that to happen. Neither the Guelfs nor the Ghibellines can be trusted to properly support the Empire. Political leaders of 1300 C.E. need to realize that.

"The Empire needs to be supported, but it is not being supported.

"You have two questions. I have already answered your first question. Your second question is this: Why am I showing myself to you on this planet that is often hidden from Humankind because it is so close to the Sun?

"This small planet is Mercury. The souls, including myself, who appear before you here were too concerned about lasting fame and so we are not to be found higher in Paradise.

"It is fitting for us souls to be found on Mercury because it is a planet that is often obscured by the Sun. It is much easier to see Venus in the sky — it is the Morning Star and the Evening Star. We souls wanted fame, but now the Sun and Venus often overshadow the planet we are associated with. Of course, we are really in the Mystic Empyrean, but we appear here as a courtesy to you.

"We did good works in the living world. The codification of the Roman law is a task that God wanted to be done. However, I and the other souls were too concerned about achieving Earthly fame while we performed our good works.

"All of us are happy. We see that we have received justice. We see that God doles out in proper proportion the fitting reward for each soul's merit. We are in Paradise.

"Many voices blend together harmoniously. We souls help to produce the harmony that is seen among the heavenly Spheres.

"One of the souls here is Romeo di Villeneuve, a person who did great deeds, but whose great deeds went unrewarded. The name 'Romeo' means 'a pilgrim to Rome.'

"Romeo was not nobly born, but he was able to get husbands for the four daughters of a count named Raymond Berenger; in fact, each daughter married a king or the brother of a king. These are the daughters and the nobles they married:

"Margaret married Louis IX (Saint Louis).

"Eleanor married Henry III of England.

"Sancha married Richard of Cornwall (the brother of Henry III of England).

"Beatrice married Charles I of Anjou.

"However, because of Romeo's success other people envied him, and he lost his position. Romeo then begged for his bread in exile.

"The world praises Romeo, but if the world knew what was in Romeo's heart as he begged, the world would praise him more."

Dante thought, *The stories of Romeo, who is in Paradise, and of Pier delle Vigne, who is among the suicides in the Inferno, are similar.*

Both Romeo and Pier lost their positions due to the envy of other people.

However, Romeo's response to losing his position was much different from the response of Pier delle Vigne. Pier, of course, committed suicide, but Romeo went begging for his bread.

Pier delle Vigne is the negative example — how not to react to political misfortune. Romeo is the positive example — how to properly respond to political misfortune.

Note also a reversal. Pier praised Holy Roman Emperor Frederick II. Here we have a Byzantine Emperor — Justinian — praising Romeo di Villeneuve.

Beatrice thought, *Learn from this, Dante. You will be in exile soon, and you will need to taste other people's bread rather than commit suicide.*

Chapter 7: Mercury — The Mystery of Redemption

Justinian sang in a mixture of Hebrew and Latin, "Hosanna, holy God of hosts, whose brightness illuminates these realms' blessed fires." Song is one of the arts found in Paradise; dance is another. Justinian's soul began to dance, and the other souls joined him — the one who performed the tasks of both Emperor and Lawgiver — in the dance. Then the souls sped away and disappeared.

Dante was silent, but inwardly he was thinking, *Speak! Speak! Beatrice is always willing to truthfully answer your questions.*

But Dante was still in awe of Beatrice. Even the mention of one syllable of her name — "Be" or "trice" — made him lower his head.

But Beatrice knew what he was thinking, and she smiled at him. Dante thought, *Such a smile would make happy even a man who was about to be burned alive.*

Beatrice said to Dante, "I know that you have a question: How can just vengeance be justly avenged?

"You know that during the reign of the Roman Emperor Tiberius, Jesus Christ was crucified. This was just vengeance for the sin of Adam.

"You also know that in 70 C.E., Titus, who later became a Roman Emperor, conquered and destroyed Jerusalem. This was just vengeance for the death of Christ.

"How can just vengeance be required for a previous just vengeance?

"Listen carefully. This is important.

"Adam sinned. He was allowed to eat all of the fruit of the Garden of Eden except the fruit of the Tree of Knowledge of Good and Evil. He was asked to restrain his free will in this one matter only, but he ate the forbidden fruit. Because he ate the forbidden fruit, he was cast out of the Garden of Eden and so were Eve and every human being after them.

"Because of Adam's sin, all Humankind was sick with sin. This illness continued for centuries. But Jesus — the Word of God — descended from Paradise to Earth.

"On Earth, Jesus added a nature to His nature. Jesus' nature is divine, but to that nature he added a second nature: the human nature that had rebelled in the Garden of Eden. In doing so, he became fully divine and fully human.

"When the human nature was joined with Jesus' divine nature, the human nature became pure and good, just as it was in the Garden of Eden before the rebellion.

"However, the human nature that was not joined to Jesus' divine nature deserved to be kicked out of the Garden of Eden because of sin.

"Jesus was crucified. If we think of the Crucifixion as punishment of the human nature, the Crucifixion was entirely just and deserved.

"But if we think of the Crucifixion as punishment of Jesus' divine nature, the Crucifixion was entirely unjust and undeserved.

"One Crucifixion occurred, but it had two different results. The Crucifixion pleased God because it paid the penalty for the sin of Adam and of Humankind. The Crucifixion also pleased a few Jews living at that time because it got rid of a Person they hated.

"The Crucifixion of Christ was just and unjust. The unjust part of the Crucifixion needed to be justly avenged. The just vengeance occurred with the destruction of Jerusalem in 70 C.E.

"The debt for Adam's sin has been paid. No one should treat Humankind badly today because of what Adam did a long time ago. That debt was paid long ago, and no one owes it today.

"The debt for the unjust Crucifixion of Jesus has been paid. No one should treat Jews badly today because of what a few Jews did a long time ago. That debt was paid long ago, and no one owes it today.

"Of course, the Romans also played a role in the Crucifixion of Jesus. No one should plan a trip to Rome today so that they can slap a few Italians around.

"But now I see that you have another question. You wonder this: Why did God choose this way to pay the penalty owed by Humankind? Why did God become incarnate knowing that He would be crucified? Why didn't God choose another way to redeem Humankind?

"Souls in Paradise know the answer. They have the inner sight and the love that enables them to know the answer.

"Many people still on Earth have tried to answer the question, but they aim arrows that miss the target. Therefore, let me explain why God's way of redeeming Humankind was the best way.

"God is perfect. Among God's perfections is omnibenevolence. God never sins. In God can be found this eternal beauty, as well as the other eternal beauties.

"God is also a Creator. What he creates directly is eternal, and it bears His mark. Among the things He creates directly are Angels, Adam and Eve, and the souls of human beings.

"The things that God directly creates have free will. God's secondary creations have no choice but to obey the laws of physics and other sciences and nature.

"The things that God directly creates resemble Him and please Him. God has given them gifts: free will and the immortality of the soul. God creates these things without sin.

"Sin, however, takes away Humankind's free will and Humankind's resemblance to God. God's glory is seen in the entire universe. In some places His glory can be seen more clearly. In some places His glory can be seen less clearly. Sin makes God's glory less visible in Humankind.

"By sinning, Humankind loses dignity in favor of illicit joy. The only way to win back that dignity is by paying the price for sinning. This is Justice.

"When Adam sinned, Humankind lost the Garden of Eden, and it lost Paradise. Sinning results in the loss of free will; a habitual sinner becomes a slave to sin. If Adam had not sinned, he would have been able to stay in the Garden of Eden and never die. By sinning, he brought the experience of death to human beings.

"How could Humankind be able to pay the debt it owed because of sin? Through two ways.

"First, God could simply forgive the sin. No payment required. This is Mercy.

"Second, Humankind could — if possible — make amends for sinning. This would be Justice.

"Listen carefully.

"Given the limits of Humankind, human beings could not make amends for sin. Adam, full of the sin of pride, tried to exalt himself by disobeying God and eating the forbidden fruit. Humankind, no matter how humble it attempts to be, cannot go as low as is needed to make up for the height that Adam attempted to climb. Therefore, Humankind cannot atone for this sin without the help of God.

"And so God helped Humankind atone for this sin.

"God could have helped Humankind through Justice alone or through Mercy alone, but God chose to help Humankind through both Justice and Mercy.

"God's incarnation and crucifixion is an act of omnibenevolence. It redeemed Humankind. From the first day of Creation until Judgment Day, no act can be as lofty or as magnificent.

"God helped Humankind through Mercy because He forgave the debt without requiring Humankind to pay it.

"God helped Humankind through Justice because the debt was repaid — Jesus on the Cross paid it. Jesus' human nature was appropriately crucified to pay Humankind's debt to God.

"Now let me explain a point that has arisen in my talk.

"You are thinking that God created the universe, and yet the things that are in the universe — things made of the elements — are perishable. They last for a while, and then they decay.

"As I have said, the things that God directly created — such as the Angels — will never go out of existence.

"However, the laws of nature act on the matter and energy that is in the universe and change them, and so these are indirect creations of God, and they are therefore not immortal.

"Remember that God directly created your soul, and so it is immortal.

"Also remember that God directly created the body of Adam and the body of Eve. This means that on the Day of Judgment, your body will be resurrected.

"Remember these things:

"Everything that God makes, such as Angels, is incorruptible and will not decay."

"Your soul is given to you directly by God. It is therefore immortal.

"God directly made the bodies of your first parents: Adam and Eve. Therefore, your body will be resurrected."

Chapter 8: Venus — Charles Martel

The ancient Greeks and Romans believed that the goddess Venus infected Humankind with violent passion and so they offered sacrifices to her. And not just her, but also to her mother, Dione. And to her son, Cupid, who they believed had taken the shape of Ascanius, Aeneas' son, and as he lay in her lap, had infected Dido, the Queen of Carthage, with passion for Aeneas.

Therefore, the ancients took Venus' name and gave it to the planet that seems to woo the Sun as it stays close to it in Venus' guises as the Evening Star and the Morning Star.

Dante was not conscious of rising through the Heavens, but he knew that he had arrived on Venus when he looked at Beatrice and saw that she had grown more beautiful. The closer she came to God, the more beautiful she became.

Dante saw lights — souls — in the light of Venus, the bright and beautiful planet. He distinguished the lights just as he could distinguish sparks in a fire or just as he could distinguish between voices when two voices are singing the same note and one of the voices starts to sing a different note.

The lights were moving at different speeds that varied according to how each soul reflected God's glory. Lightning is fast, but each of these lights was faster than lightning as they came closer to Dante and Beatrice. The lights had been dancing in the Mystic Empyrean among the highest order of Angels — the Seraphim — but they had consented to appear before Dante and educate him.

Song and dance are present in Paradise. The souls in front sang "Hosanna" so sweetly that for years afterward Dante longed to hear it again.

One soul came close to Dante and Beatrice and said, "We are all ready to serve you and make you joyful. We have appeared together on this, the third Sphere, to serve you. You once wrote a poem that began, 'Oh, you whose intelligence moves the Third Sphere of the Heavens.'

"We are filled with love, and we will happily stop here and stay with you for a while."

Dante looked at Beatrice, who was filled with joy and who nodded at him to give him her approval of his asking the soul questions, and then he looked at the light who had spoken to him and asked, gently, "Who are you?"

The light who was a soul glowed more brightly and more beautifully because he was happy to serve Dante.

The soul said, "I lived for only a few years on Earth. If I had lived longer, I would have been able to avert much trouble that will afflict Earth.

"I know that you cannot see me. All you can see is this light that envelops me. This light is happiness. I am enveloped in it the way a silkworm envelops itself in silk.

"Although you cannot see me, you knew me when I was alive on Earth. We were friends. If I had lived, you would have seen much more of my friendship for you instead of just its beginning.

"My grandfather, Charles I, acquired Provence through marriage. My father, Charles II of Naples, would have passed it on to me. I also would have been heir to the Kingdom of Naples and the Kingdom of Apulia. I became King of Hungary in 1290. I would have been the ruler of Sicily except that the bad rule of my family — the House of Anjou — caused the Sicilians to rebel in the Sicilian Vespers of 30 March 1282. The Sicilians cried out against the House of Anjou, 'Death, death to them!' Because of the Sicilians' uprising, the crown of Sicily passed from the House of Anjou to the House of Aragon."

Dante thought, *This is my friend Charles Martel, a French Angevin Prince. He died young at age 24 in a cholera epidemic. He visited Florence for a few weeks in 1294, one year before he died, and he and I knew and liked each other.*

One need not spend a lot of time climbing the Mountain of Purgatory. Some souls spend centuries climbing the mountain, but Charles Martel died only five years ago and already his soul is in Paradise.

Charles Martel continued, "Robert of Anjou, my brother, who will one day be King of Naples, needs to wise up. His rule is poor. Although his and my father was liberal, Robert is stingy. Working under him are men who care most for filling chests up with gold. My family has contained many good people and good rulers, but it has also contained many bad people and bad rulers."

Dante said, "I am happy to see you again, friend, and I am happy to see that you are in Paradise. I am also happy that you know how happy I am. As a saved soul in Paradise, you know about my happiness because you can read it in the place where all good begins and ends: the mind of God.

"You have made me happy; now I ask that you make me wise. Please answer these questions: How can a good father produce a bad son? How can good parents produce bad children? You have said that Charles, your father, was generous. Yet Robert, your brother, is not generous. It would seem that a generous father would produce a generous son. It would also seem that a greedy father would produce a greedy son."

Charles Martel replied, "I will try to explain this to you. First, let me clear up a false belief. People of our time believed that the stars and planets influenced our characters and our lives. They also believed that Providence influenced our characters and our lives through influencing the stars and planets.

"A later age will know that the stars and planets have no influence on us at all; astrology is not a science. Of course, God is important to us. For one thing, God created us and the universe, and God keeps the universe and us in existence. If not for God, nothing would exist.

"In addition, God created such things as sex, heredity, and — as a later age will learn — something called evolution. When God created the universe, He created the physical laws that govern the universe. In a later age, Catholic nuns will do things right. They will teach evolution in science class, and they will teach creation in religion class.

"God knew that human beings would be different, and He wanted them to be different. They have individual characteristics and potential capabilities. These individual characteristics and potential capabilities are needed in society. Neither God nor society wants all human beings to be exactly alike. Different human beings are capable of doing different things, and different things are needed to make a functioning society.

"Through inheriting different traits passed down from both male and female ancestors, humans are born with potentialities that can be developed — or not developed — through environment and education and the use of free will in making choices.

"It is not the case that nobility of character is always passed on from a noble father or mother to a child. The nobility of character is acquired in part through the characteristics and potential capabilities that one inherits, and in part through education and environment, but mainly it is acquired — or not acquired — through choices freely made. The most important choice that anyone can make is whether to be a good person or a bad person. A good father can have a good and/or a bad son. A bad father can have a good and/or a bad son. Good parents can have good and/or bad children. Bad parents can have good and/or bad children.

"God's laws of heredity work well. Without them, chaos would reign. God knows what He is doing. Do I need to say more?"

Dante replied, "No. God cannot fail, and God created the physical laws of the universe."

Charles Martel asked, "If no social order existed, would this be good for Humankind?"

Dante replied, "No. Obviously, social order is needed."

Charles Martel asked, "Do human beings need different characteristics and different capabilities in order to have a functioning society? According to the ancient Greek philosopher Aristotle, different characteristics and different capabilities are necessary in order to have a functioning society.

"Many characteristics and capabilities are needed. One man is born with the potential to be a giver of laws, as was Solon, who gave laws to Athens and who was one of the Seven Sages of Greece. Another man is born with the potential to be a king and war leader, as was Xerxes, King of Persia and leader of armies. Another man is born with the potential to be a priest, as was Melchizedek, whom Genesis identified as 'the priest of the most high God.' Another man is born with the potential to be a mechanic, as was Daedalus, who was imprisoned with his son, Icarus. To escape, Daedalus built wings for himself and his son. But in the mythic story, Icarus flew too near the Sun, the wax melted and released the feathers, and Icarus fell into the sea and drowned.

"Nature gives potential to humans without regard to familial status. A great son can be born to a base father, and a base son can be born to a great father. The same is true for females.

"Good parents can produce bad children. Bad parents can produce good children. The children can be very different from each other even when they share the same parents.

"Esau and Jacob were twins, but they were very different. Esau was a hunter in the fields, but Jacob lived in tents.

"Look at Romulus, the co-founder of Rome with his brother, Remus. His father was not royal or aristocratic, but Romulus' deeds were so notable that people could not believe that his father was basely born, and so they believed that Romulus' father was Mars, the Roman god of war.

"Now that you understand this, let me make a further point. One's characteristics and potential capabilities ought to be suitable for one's life work. If a person has characteristics and potential capabilities that are not suited to the kind of work that person does, that person will fail.

"Society should pay attention to this. If it did, both society and individual human beings would be better off.

"Unfortunately, a person who has the characteristics and potential capabilities to be a warrior is forced to be a priest, and a person who has the characteristics and potential capabilities to be a priest is forced to be a king.

"All too often, people find themselves doing work that they are not suited to do and that could be much better done by someone else."

Chapter 9: Venus — Cuanza, Folquet, Rahab

Dante the Poet thought, *Clemence of Hapsburg, your husband Charles Martel told me prophecies of plots against you and your relatives. But he told me, "Don't reveal the specifics of what I have said. Let time pass and reveal the plots." Because I gave him this promise, I can say only that those who harm you will regret it.*

But now that soul who was Charles Martel looked at the Sun. This saved soul looked at the Eternal Good, but living human beings too often look away from the Eternal Good.

And now another light came toward Dante. This saved soul glowed with the prospect of helping him.

Beatrice looked at Dante and nodded, giving her assent to his desire to speak with the saved soul.

Dante said to the saved soul, "Blessed soul, you know my thoughts because you can see into the mind of God, and God knows my thoughts. Therefore, you know my questions. Please answer them."

The saved soul, who received joy from giving joyously to others, replied, "I lived in the March of Treviso, and my family castle was located on the hill of Romano. My mother dreamed of a burning torch before she gave birth to Ezzelino III, my brother, who was a bloodthirsty tyrant who now stands deep in the boiling river of blood in the Inferno.

"My name is Cunizza, and I appear to you here on Venus because much of my life before I repented was filled with excessive sexual desire."

Dante thought, *Cunizza, who died in 1279, is the sister of the tyrant Ezzelino, who died in 1259 and who is in the Inferno because of the blood he spilled when he was tyrant. Cunizza was the lover of Sordello, one of the late repentant in Prepurgatory. She left her husband for him. She had lots of husbands and lovers, and she had lots of sex. Cunizza fell in love easily. Of course, she still had free will and the ability to tell right from wrong. In later life, she was a good person and did many good deeds. Sinners can repent and end up in Paradise.*

Cunizza continued, "I had many husbands and lovers while I was alive, but I repented. I can recall my sins, but I have drunk from the stream Lethe, and I do not feel the sting of my sins. All I feel is forgiveness, both forgiveness by God and forgiveness by myself. Gladly I forgive the excessive love that I had because when I repented, my excessive passionate love became *caritas*: love for all Humankind and for God. We saved souls in Paradise do not beat ourselves up because of our sins. We know that God has forgiven us, and we forgive ourselves.

"This soul beside me has left great fame behind on Earth. His fame will last 500 years. A person who achieves excellence in the living world can achieve a fame that will remain as a second life after the person's physical body has died.

"And yet this soul's remembered excellence means nothing to the people who live between the Tagliamento and the Adige rivers in Italy. These people do not repent. Not even war and the threat of war makes them repent.

"Let me make prophecies: The blood of Paduans will flow because they refuse to do what they ought to do."

Beatrice thought, *In 1314, Can Grande della Scala will defeat the Paduans outside Vicenza. The Paduans should, but do not, have allegiance to the Empire.*

Cunizza continued, "An arrogant man reigns in Treviso; his fate has already been decided."

Beatrice thought, *Rizzardo da Cammino, the arrogant Lord of Treviso, will be murdered in 1312 while he plays chess.*

Cunizza continued, "The godless shepherd of Feltro will commit a crime so great that the Malta, a papal prison near Lake Bolsena, has never held a criminal as bad as he. The Ferraran blood that he will spill would fill a vast vat. He will spill it only to prove that he is loyal to his party. Such actions will become common in that region."

Beatrice thought, *In 1314, a group of Ghibelline refugees will become the guests of Alessandro Novella, the Bishop of Feltro, a Guelf who will treacherously turn them over to their enemies, who will behead them.*

Cunizza continued, "My words may seem harsh, but they are justified by their truth."

She then joined the other souls, and they danced.

The soul who had been beside Cunizza and whose excellence and fame she had mentioned now glowed brightly red, like sunlight shining through a ruby.

Joy makes souls in Paradise bright. Joy makes living people smile. No joy is in the Inferno, only dark minds.

Dante said to the soul who was glowing red, "God can see all, and you can see into the mind of God, and therefore you know every thought I have. Why wait, then, to answer my questions? If our positions were reversed, I certainly would quickly answer your questions."

The saved soul replied, "I lived in a country on the Mediterranean: France. In particular, I lived in Marseilles. My name is Folquet. Some people still remember my name."

Dante thought, *Folquet, who died in 1231, was a famous troubadour. Later in life, he became a Cistercian monk, and then he became the Bishop of Toulouse. He was a gifted poet.*

Folquet continued, "In life, I loved passionately, and so I appear to you here on Venus. My passionate love on Earth rivaled that of famous lovers.

"The passionate love I felt rivaled that of Dido, Queen of Carthage. Pygmalion, Dido's brother, killed her husband, Sichaeus, and she fled to North Africa, where she founded Carthage. Aeneas, blown off course by a storm sent by Juno, landed at Carthage, and Dido fell in love with him although she had pledged to remain faithful to her husband. Dido and Aeneas had a love affair until Jupiter, through Mercury, reminded Aeneas that he had a destiny to fulfill in Italy: to become an important ancestor of the Roman people. Out of grief, Dido committed suicide. Dido wronged both Sichaeus, her late husband, and Creusa, Aeneas' late wife, who had died during the fall of Troy. Dido is in the Inferno among the lustful.

"The passionate love I felt rivaled that of Phyllis, a Thracian princess who loved Demophoön, the son of Theseus. They were supposed to be married, but when he did not show up at the altar, she hanged herself.

"The passionate love I felt rivaled that of Deianira, the wife of Hercules. He fell out of love with her and pursued Iole instead. She believed that a shirt soaked in the blood of Nessus, a Centaur (who had tried to rape her, but whom Hercules killed) would restore Hercules' love for her. Nessus had told her that, but he tricked her. His blood was like acid to Hercules, and Hercules killed himself to escape the agony that the Centaur's blood caused him. Deianira also killed herself. Nessus is in the Inferno. He is one of the guards at the river of boiling blood.

"But I and the other saved souls you see here repented while we were alive, and so we have no need to repent here. Instead, we smile here because we know that God has forgiven us. God wants all human beings to repent on Earth so that He can forgive them.

"All of us souls appear to you here on Venus, whose Sphere is the last that the shadow of the Earth touches. According to your medieval beliefs, the Earth is at the center of the universe, and around it are the Spheres containing the Moon, Mercury, Venus, the Sun, and so on. Imagine the Sun's rays striking the Earth. The Earth casts a shadow that is cone-shaded. The Earth's shadow sometimes envelopes the Moon in an eclipse and is large enough to envelop Mercury and touches the Sphere in which is Venus. God is doing you a favor by letting the universe appear to you in accordance with your medieval beliefs. A later age will know that the Sun is at the center of the solar system and that Mercury, Venus, and the Earth orbit the Sun. But God the Creator can make the universe appear to you in the way you expect it to appear. That way, you will not be overwhelmed with too much new information and will be able to retain more of the important information, such as that given to you by us saved souls who appear to you in these Spheres but who are really in the Mystic Empyrean with God.

"But now let me answer a question that I know you have. You wish to know the identity of this soul by me. This soul glows like crystal water through which sunshine streams.

"This soul was the first to rise out of Limbo when Christ harrowed Hell. This is Rahab, who was once the whore of Jericho. Joshua sent two spies to Jericho, Rahab allowed them to enter her house, and when soldiers came looking for the two spies, she hid them under bundles of flax on the roof of her house. The two spies promised that she and her family would be spared when Joshua's soldiers conquered the city if she would hang a red cord out of a window of her house. The two spies and Jacob's soldiers kept that promise.

"Rahab helped make possible Joshua's first conquest in the Holy Land, an area of the world in which Pope Boniface VIII seems to have little interest.

"Your own city, Florence, was founded by Lucifer and by Mars, the god of war. Your city creates flowers of gold — the gold coins that are the Florentine florins — and these golden flowers turn priests and popes who should be shepherds into wolves that prey on the sheep that shepherds should protect.

"Those who should study the Gospel and other books of the Bible ignore them. People study Canon Law and make notes in the margins, but they engage in this study only so they can make money.

"The Pope and the Cardinals think only about making money. They do not think about Nazareth, where the Angel Gabriel opened his wings at the Annunciation to Mary.

"But the Vatican and other places in Rome where flowed the blood of martyrs who gave their lives for God will soon be free of this adulterous passion for gold."

Beatrice thought, *Here and on the previous planets, we saw souls who were associated with a planet for negative reasons. The shadow of the Earth touched and corrupted these Spheres. First, the souls seen on the Moon did not keep their religious vows. Second, the souls seen on Mercury were excessively concerned about Earthly fame. Finally, the souls seen on Venus are those who took passionate love to an extreme. On the Sun and on the other planets we have yet to visit, the souls we will see will be associated with these Spheres for a positive reason — for something they had and have rather than for something they lacked.*

Chapter 10: Sun — Saint Thomas Aquinas

God the Father is the Creator. The Son is the Word of God. Together, they breathe forth the Essence of Love, aka the Holy Ghost. Throughout the universe, signs of the Creator can be seen and felt.

God the Creator loves His creation and contemplates it.

Consider for a moment the planet Earth and the Sun. Imagine that the equator forms a wheel that extends into space. Imagine that the orbit of the Earth around the Sun (or, as Dante the Pilgrim believed, imagine that the orbit of the Sun around the Earth) forms a wheel.

The two wheels meet. Sometimes the Sun is above the equator, and sometimes the Sun is below the equator. This causes the seasons.

This relationship is absolutely correct. If the Sun were sometimes way above the equator and sometimes way below the equator, the Earth's seasons would be extreme. If the Sun stayed always above the equator and did not move, the Earth's seasons would always stay the same and would not change. The relationship of the parts and the whole is absolutely correct for seasons that will support life on Earth.

The universe is a great work of art, and we should contemplate it. God contemplates His own creation, and we should likewise contemplate it.

Pay attention to the above. It is important. What is to come is also important.

Dante was in the Sun with Beatrice. Dante had not been aware that he was rising to the Sun until he was in the Sun, just like he is not aware that a thought is coming until he has that thought.

As before, Beatrice guided their ascent, which took place instantaneously.

The Sun is the brightest thing that living human beings can see, but Dante saw saved souls on the Sun who were brighter than the Sun. In Paradise, the brightness of saved souls surpasses the brightness of the Sun.

No genius, no art, and no skill is capable of showing living human beings how bright are the saved souls of Paradise. Living people on Earth must make it to Paradise and experience this for themselves. The saved souls constantly experience God, and they constantly experience bliss.

Beatrice said to Dante, "Give thanks to God, Who is the Sun to Angels, by Whose grace you have arrived at the Sun."

Hearing Beatrice, Dante readily and willingly and enthusiastically gave thanks to God. He thanked God so strongly that he even forgot Beatrice.

This pleased Beatrice. She smiled, and Dante saw her beauty and became aware of his surroundings.

Lights who were saved souls circled Beatrice and Dante. They were like the halo of light that sometimes surrounds Latona's daughter: Diana, aka the Moon. They were like a crown for Dante and Beatrice.

The saved souls sang as they circled them, and that song is one of the delights awaiting the repentant after they die and go to Paradise.

The lights circled Dante and Beatrice three times and then stopped. They were like dancing ladies who stopped so they could listen to new notes and catch a new rhythm.

One of the saved souls spoke to Dante: "You are blessed by God, who kindles true love that increases the more it loves. You have been allowed to ascend into Paradise. From Paradise, no one descends unless they will later ascend again."

Beatrice thought, *Saint Paul was allowed to visit Paradise before he died. Of course, he returned to Paradise after he died. Dante will return to Paradise after he dies. He is saved.*

The saved soul continued, "Because God has shown His grace to you, we will of course help you by giving you information. None of us saved souls would refuse to give your thirsty soul wine from a flask; that would be like a moving stream refusing to move to the sea.

"I know that you want to know who these souls are who are the flowers in the crown around this lady who is your guide.

"I am a Dominican friar. Saint Dominic led me and many others along a path where all may be fed if they do not stray from the path. I am Thomas Aquinas."

Beatrice thought, *Thomas Aquinas was born in 1224, and he died at age 50 in 1274. Dante was born in 1265, so he was nine years old when Thomas Aquinas died. Thomas Aquinas will become Saint Thomas Aquinas in 1323, two years after Dante will die. Thomas Aquinas is much respected now, in 1300, but he will be much more respected later. He will be the dominant Catholic theologian. He will be regarded as the greatest medieval philosopher. Saint Thomas believed in both revealed truth, such as the revelations that we have in sacred scripture, and in discovered truth, such as we find by using our reason. He argued that the two kinds of truth were compatible. Moses Maimonides, a great Jewish thinker, believed the same thing.*

In this first circle are 12 souls, and they surround Dante and me like the numbers on a clock. All of the 12 souls are male. Later, a second circle of 12 souls will join the first circle. The number 24 is important in the Bible — for example, in the Book of Revelation there are 24 elders.

Thomas Aquinas continued, "I will tell you about the other souls. Look at each soul as I explain who the soul is. This soul to my right is my teacher, Albert of Cologne, aka Albertus Magnus, aka Albert the Great."

Beatrice thought, *Albert the Great died in 1280, and he will be canonized in 1931. Albert the Great is known as the Universal Doctor, a name that reflects his great knowledge. He commented widely on the ancient Greek philosopher Aristotle. Like Thomas Aquinas, Albert the Great was a Dominican. Thomas Aquinas went to Cologne in 1248 to study under him.*

Thomas Aquinas continued, "The next soul is Gratian, who smiles brightly. He served well in two courts of law, and Paradise is happy to welcome him."

Beatrice thought, *Gratian is Italian. He was a Benedictine monk, and he is known as the father of canon law. Gratian sought to harmonize Church and civil laws, thereby allowing canon law to be correctly interpreted. His* magnum opus *is* A Concordance of Discordant Regulations, *or* Gratian's Decretals, *which appeared between 1140 and 1150. Dante finds it interesting that he sees Gratian here. One of Dante's criticisms of the Catholic Church is that it does not spend enough time studying scripture; instead, it spends too much time studying Church law. Yet here he sees Gratian, the great compiler of Church law. What can he learn from this? He can learn that Church law is important, but all of us have to be careful to use it well, neither overvaluing nor undervaluing it.*

Thomas Aquinas continued, "The next soul is Peter. Like the poor widow, he offered what he had to the Church."

Beatrice thought, *Peter Lombard lived in the 12th century, and he was the bishop of Paris. He wrote* Libri Sententiarum, *aka* The Books of Opinions, *which brought together the opinions of the Church fathers on four key subjects: the Godhead, the incarnation, creation, and the sacraments. Peter Lombard called his writings his "widow's mite," a reference to the New Testament story (Luke 21:1-4), about a widow who brought her small offering to the temple. This is the story: "And Jesus looked up, and saw the rich men casting their gifts into the treasury. And he saw also a certain poor widow casting in thither the small amount of two mites. And Jesus said, 'Of a truth I say to you, that this poor widow has cast in more than they all: For all these have of their abundance cast in to the offerings of God: but she of her penury has cast in all the living that she had.'"*

Thomas Aquinas continued, "The fifth light is the most beautiful of all of us. His love was passionate, as can be seen in his 'Song of Songs.' Because of his passionate love, people debated whether he is in Paradise or in the Inferno. He is the wisest of all, and no one has as much wisdom as he has. A second person has never arisen with as much wisdom as Solomon had."

Beatrice thought, *This wise soul is Solomon, David's son by Bathsheba. Though Saint Augustine believed that King Solomon was damned, Solomon is the most beautiful in this group. Solomon had a dream in which God asked him what he wanted, and Solomon wanted wisdom: "an understanding heart to judge Your people, that I may discern between good and bad" (I Kings 3:9). God granted him that, as well as other things that Solomon did not ask for. Solomon used his wisdom to resolve a dispute between two women who both claimed to be the mother of a living baby. He ordered the child to be cut in half, and each mother to be given half of the child. One of the women spoke up and asked Solomon to give the child to the other woman. The other woman remained silent. Solomon knew that the woman who had spoken up is the real mother of the child because the real mother would not want the child killed.*

Thomas Aquinas continued, "The soul next to him knew, while he was in the living world, what an Angel is and what an Angel does."

Beatrice thought, *This soul is Dionysius the Areopagite. In the 1st century, Saint Paul converted an Athenian named Dionysius the Areopagite (Acts 17:34). People incorrectly believed that Dionysius the Areopagite had written a highly influential book about Angels titled* On the Heavenly Hierarchy, *aka* The Celestial Hierarchy. *He did not write that book, but as Thomas Aquinas said about him, while he was in the living world, he knew what an Angel is and what an Angel does.*

Thomas Aquinas continued, "Inside this light, which is tiny, is the great defender of the Christian age. Saint Augustine used his words."

Beatrice thought, *This soul is Paulus Orosius, who was a Spanish cleric and historian. He was a 5th-century contemporary of Saint Augustine. Some pagans believed that the arrival of Christianity had made the world worse than it had been, so Orosius wrote seven books opposing that belief. These books were called* Seven Books of History Against the Pagans.

Thomas Aquinas continued, "You must be eager to know who this light, the eighth, is. This soul, who is now in the realm of all good, experienced much evil on Earth. He was martyred, and his remains are now at the Church of Saint Peter in Pavia, which is in Lombardy."

Beatrice thought, *This soul is Boethius, a Roman, who wrote* On the Consolation of Philosophy *while he was in prison. In 524 C.E., he was executed for treason — although he was innocent — after he completed the book. After my body died, Dante read* On the Consolation of Philosophy *and was consoled by it. Boethius is also known as Saint Severinus; his full name was Anicius Manlius Severinus Boethius.*

Thomas Aquinas continued, "The next soul is Isidore."

Beatrice thought, *Isidore of Seville was a Spaniard who died in 636 C.E. He wrote a highly influential encyclopedia of the scientific knowledge of his time.*

Thomas Aquinas continued, "The next soul is Bede."

Beatrice thought, *The Venerable Bede, an Anglo-Saxon monk who died in 735 C.E., is known as the father of English history. He wrote the five-volume* Ecclesiastical History of the English Nation.

Thomas Aquinas continued, "The next soul is Richard, who is known for his contemplations."

Beatrice thought, *Richard of Saint Victor died in 1173 C.E. He was called the Great Contemplator after he wrote a book titled* De Contemplatione. *He was an important 12th-century mystic, and he was prior of the illustrious Augustinian monastery at Saint Victor near Paris.*

Thomas Aquinas continued, "This soul is Siger, who mourned the length of his mortal life. He taught at the University of Paris, before which was the Rue de Fouarre, aka the Street of Straw. He taught truths for which he was hated."

Beatrice thought, *This soul is Siger of Brabant, who was a Belgian whose beliefs opposed those of Saint Thomas. For example, Siger thought that the world could have always existed. He also doubted that the soul is immortal — since he is in Paradise, he has happily discovered that he was wrong about that. He and*

And now the wheel of souls moved the way a clock moves, and the souls sang a song. Parts moved together, in harmony, as in the act of creation. Parts made a whole, and God's Bride was with the Bridegroom. Joy and eternity were one.

Chapter 11: Sun — Saint Thomas Aquinas Praises Saint Francis of Assisi

Dante the Poet thought, *People pursue many activities in such a way that keeps them rooted to the Earth rather than helping them to rise to Paradise. Some people seek to rise to material gain in law. Some people seek to rise to material gain in medicine. Some people seek to benefit by acquiring religious sinecures. Some people seek to rise to political power by using force or fraud. Some people plan thefts. Some people seek to rise to material gain by planning affairs of state. Some people seek the pleasures of the flesh. Some people are lazy.*

But I did not worry about such things because I was magnificently welcomed to Paradise with Beatrice.

The saved souls were dancing, and when each soul had returned to the place it had been before the dance started, they stopped dancing and stood still like candles in a circular chandelier.

Thomas Aquinas said to Dante, "I reflect the rays of God, and I look into God's mind and I see your thoughts. I see that you are perplexed by some of the things I said. You want me to speak plainly and clearly and explain the things that perplex you.

"Two things perplex you. One, I said, 'Saint Dominic led me and many others along a path where all may be fed if they do not stray from the path.' And two, I said, 'A second person has never arisen with as much wisdom as Solomon had.' I must speak more clearly.

"The wisdom of Providence is so great that living human beings cannot understand it. But be aware that Providence wants the Church, aka the Bride of Christ, to be able to go to her Bridegroom, aka Christ, with her faithfulness and goodness intact, and so Providence sent two princes to reform her and make her well again.

"One reformer on Earth was like one of the Seraphim, the highest order of Angels, who are symbolic of the highest love for God. This reformer stressed repentance of one's sins to make oneself closer to God.

"The other reformer on Earth was like one of the Cherubim, the second highest order of Angels, who are symbolic of the highest kind of wisdom. This reformer stressed getting doctrine right.

"The Church needed — and needs — to be reformed, and these two saints in different but complementary ways sought to reform it. Saint Francis stressed repentance of one's sins to make oneself closer to God. Saint Dominic stressed getting doctrine right. Praise of one of the reformers is also praise for the other reformer because both reformers had the same goal in mind: Reform the Church to make it stronger.

"I myself will speak of only one reformer."

Dante the Pilgrim thought, *The two great reformers of the 13th century were Saint Francis of Assisi and Saint Dominic. Saint Dominic is from Spain, and Saint Francis is from Italy. Saint Dominic's focus is on the gifts of the mind, and Saint Francis' focus is on the gifts of the heart. A proper Church needs both wisdom and love. Thomas Aquinas is a Dominican friar, so I expect him to talk about Saint Dominic.*

Thomas Aquinas continued, "In Assisi was born a reformer. The name 'Assisi' can be interpreted as 'A man has arisen,' but a more accurate name would be 'Orient,' or 'A Sun has arisen.'"

Dante the Pilgrim thought, *I was wrong. Thomas Aquinas, a Dominican friar, is going to speak about Saint Francis of Assisi. He has said enough that I know that he will praise Saint Francis. Saint Francis was a wandering saint. He took vows of chastity, poverty, and obedience. He was a missionary who visited parts of the world devoted to Islam. Thomas Aquinas is not against the Franciscans. He knows that the two orders of friars are on the same side. Down on Earth, I have seen these two orders of friars engage in a destructive kind of competition. That Saint Thomas is going to tell me about Saint Francis shows something about wisdom. Don't be afraid to learn from other sources and from traditions other than your own. Although Saint Thomas is a Dominican, he knows that studying the story of Saint Francis can lead to wisdom. In Paradise there is no jealousy between the Dominicans and the Franciscans because they know that they are on the same side.*

Thomas Aquinas continued, "This reformer, even as a youth, showed holiness. He even made his father angry, preferring doing that to leaving something undone for God.

"This reformer loved a certain lady, whom other people preferred to flee from as if she were death.

"This reformer even appeared in court, with his father present, to marry this lady. This reformer loved this lady more and more each day.

"This lady had been married before, and she remained unmarried for over 11 centuries before she married a second time. No one loved her for over 1100 years. She had been alone all that time.

"She had been alone although it was due to her that Amyclas, lying on a bed of seaweed, was able to be unfrightened when Julius Caesar, whose word could terrify the world, demanded to be ferried across the Adriatic Sea. Amyclas had no possessions, and therefore he did not worry about losing them.

"She had been alone although it was her who climbed up the Cross to be with Jesus while Mary remained at the foot of the Cross.

"No doubt you know of whom I am speaking. I am speaking of Saint Francis, who married Lady Poverty, whose first Bridegroom was Jesus Himself."

Dante thought, *When Saint Francis was still young, he decided to forego the pursuit of wealth and instead be poor. In figurative terms, he married Lady Poverty. Of course, Lady Poverty is not someone people normally choose to consort with. Saint Francis always wanted to do the right thing. In 1207, when Francis was 25 years old, he sold some possessions of his father — a horse and a loaf of bread — and he gave the money to a church. This enraged his father, who made Francis appear before the Bishop of Assisi. His father asked Francis to agree to forfeit his right of inheritance, and Francis gladly agreed, thus marrying Lady Poverty.*

Poverty is not necessarily a good thing. Christians and everyone else should work to relieve poverty. It is much better that all people have food, shelter, and clothing than that some people be so poor that they have to do without. If poverty has any advantage, it is that a poor person is more likely to lack pride and more likely to turn to God than a rich person is.

But voluntary poverty can be a very good thing indeed. Saint Francis chose voluntary poverty. He renounced trying to gather as much material wealth as he could so that he could do the work that God wanted him to do.

Thomas Aquinas continued, "The marriage of Saint Francis and Lady Poverty was fruitful. Soon other people became followers of Saint Francis. Saint Francis and Lady Poverty loved each other, and their love inspired other people. One such follower was Saint Bernard. He cast his shoes off and ran to follow Saint Francis, and even though he ran he thought he was slow. Giles and Sylvester also followed Saint Francis."

Dante thought, *Saint Francis and Giles were out walking when they came across a beggar woman. Saint Francis had nothing to give her, as he was wearing a simple, much-worn habit with a bit of rope for a belt. Giles, however, was wearing a coat. Saint Francis told him, "Give it to her." Giles handed the beggar woman the coat, and he became one of the first Franciscans.*

Thomas Aquinas continued, "Saint Francis had a family. He was married to Lady Poverty, and his followers were part of his family."

Beatrice thought, *In the Inferno, Brunetto Latini was unfruitful. He did speak of Dante as his son, but Brunetto Latini's doing so was a way for him to be remembered. If Dante becomes famous, and he will, then Brunetto Latini will be famous because he was a teacher or a mentor for Dante. A more fruitful family is one in which all do good work. Brunetto Latini wrote for fame, and his writings will perish except for scholars researching Dante. Saint Francis' family is still doing good work. The Franciscans still do many good deeds throughout the world, and 700 years from now they will continue to do many good deeds throughout the world.*

Thomas Aquinas continued, "Saint Francis and his family wore a humble cord for a belt. He was not ashamed that his father was Bernardine, a merchant. He appeared before Pope Innocent III, who provisionally approved the order of Saint Francis. His followers grew, and in 1123, Pope Honorarius III officially approved the order of Saint Francis.

"Then Saint Francis went to Egypt to speak before the Sultan and try to convert him. Saint Francis was hoping to be martyred."

Dante thought, *Yes, Saint Francis wanted to be martyred, but he was so likable that the Sultan treated him well.*

Thomas Aquinas continued, "Saint Francis failed to convert the Sultan, and therefore he returned to Italy. During the two years before his death, he bore the wounds of Christ. This was his final seal."

Dante thought, *Saint Francis received the stigmata. The stigmata are the wounds of Christ. These unexplained markings are on the hands and feet and on the side of the person receiving them. In Saint Francis' case, they are regarded as a miracle. The stigmata are Saint Francis' final seal. A seal, of course, is used to seal envelopes. Hot wax is dropped across the folded part of the envelope and then a seal of some kind is pressed into the wax. The seal indicates that this is a genuine letter, not a fake. Saint Francis was genuine, not a fake. The seal indicates that the letter is finished and approved. Saint Francis' life was finished and approved: He came as close to perfection as a living human being can, and he entered Paradise. Near the end of his life, Saint Francis was a fully completed work of art.*

Thomas Aquinas continued, "When Francis died, he called on his followers to love Lady Poverty. When Francis died, he loved Lady Poverty.

"What other kind of person should be a reformer like Saint Francis? Who can help the Church to keep a straight course in dangerous waters? Such a person was Saint Dominic, the leader of the order of friars to which I belong. A true follower of Saint Dominic will see riches in the hold of the ship.

"But the followers of Saint Dominic have grown greedy. They stray from the true path to untrue pastures. The farther Dominican friars get away from Saint Dominic, the less milk they bring back.

"Some Dominican friars stay close to Saint Dominic, but they are few. To make cowls for each of them would take little cloth.

"I have tried to speak plainly and to make clear to you the meaning of 'a path where all may be fed if they do not stray from the path.' I hope that you have understood me."

Beatrice thought, *You are supposed to learn from this, Dante. Like Saint Francis, you will be poor. You will also be in exile. One thing that you have to do is to choose your reaction to what happens to you. One kind of reaction is to commit suicide. That kind of reaction, of course, will get you a place in the Inferno forever: Remember Pier delle Vigne. Another kind of reaction is to embrace your fate. Saint Francis embraced poverty. Dante, you can choose to do your best in the face of poverty and exile.*

You also need to learn that wisdom is about seeing things in the right relationship. The Sun and the Earth are in the right relationship to have seasons and to support life. The Franciscans and the Dominicans need to have the right relationship, which is to be on the same side and to work for the good of the Church. The Church needs to recognize the importance of both love and wisdom.

Scholarship and wisdom are two different things, although learned scholars can be wise. Thomas Aquinas is a very learned soul here. However, Saint Francis was not known for scholarship. Nevertheless, both Thomas Aquinas and Saint Francis were and are wise. Wisdom is a broader concept than many people assume.

Let's think about the way that we accumulate knowledge. One of Humankind's greatest inventions has been writing because we can now write down what we learn. A person can study and acquire wisdom, but when that person dies, those insights can be lost unless that person has written down his or her thoughts. When a person writes a book that appears in a library, that person is making his or her insights available communally — someone else can read that book and learn those insights.

In addition, the other people who read that book can build on its insights. They can publish their own books that contain their own insights. These insights can build up over the years. For one thing, we don't need to keep reinventing the wheel generation after generation. The wheel has already been invented. New generations can figure out better ways of using the wheel.

Books have a major advantage over the oral transmission of information. In Africa, storytellers, who were called griots, passed along information orally. It was said that when a griot died, a library died. It would be much better if the griots wrote down what they know. That way, a library will not die when a griot dies.

When a person can write a good book and does not write that book, it is as if a child has died.

Still, wisdom does not mean book-learning, although book-learning is important. A person such as Saint Francis is known for his love, and love can be a kind of wisdom. Love can be a way of knowing what is important.

Chapter 12: Sun — Saint Bonaventure Praises Saint Dominic

The moment that Thomas Aquinas stopped speaking, the circle of souls began to revolve and dance again. Before it had revolved in a complete circle, a second circle of souls joined it.

Beatrice thought, *Two facts about wisdom are that it is communal and it is cumulative. We see that it is communal because these souls are in groups. We see that it is cumulative because a second group of souls has joined the first group of souls. The two wheels of souls are interacting with each other. One of the things that this means is that wisdom consists of, in part, understanding parts and wholes. Wisdom is, in part, understanding the way that things fit together and the way that things interact with each other.*

The second circle of souls interacted with the first group of souls, matching motion with motion and song with song.

The two groups fit together. They were like two rainbows — the two rainbows that appear when the goddess Juno calls Iris to appear to her. One rainbow indicates that Iris is the messenger of the gods; the other rainbow indicates Iris' double splendor when she attends to the Queen of the gods. Wisdom is doubly splendid.

The two groups fit together. They were like the voice of a caller and the voice of an echo. People of wisdom magnify and complete the voices of other people of wisdom.

The two groups fit together. They were like the rainbow that God put in the sky to assure human beings that the world will never again drown under a great flood. People of wisdom can prevent calamities and reassure human beings.

The two groups danced and sang together, and the outer circle of souls responded with love to the inner circle of souls.

The two groups ceased dancing and singing at the same moment just as two eyes will open or close at the same time according to our desire. The actions of the two groups were in harmony.

One soul from the newly arrived group of souls spoke. Dante turned to that soul; Dante was like the needle of a compass that immediately points to the North Pole and the North Star.

The saved soul spoke, "The Church has two reformers who are like the two wheels of a two-wheeled chariot. Thomas Aquinas has praised one of the reformers: Saint Francis, who was my guide. I was a Franciscan friar. Now I want to praise the other reformer: Saint Dominic. One reformer should not be mentioned without the other reformer because both sought to make the Church stronger. Both fought on the same side in the same battle. The Church needed to be reformed, and these two reformers, in different but complementary ways, rose to the challenge.

"The soldiers of the Church were few and fearful and divided although Jesus had spilled His blood for them, so God the Father sent the Church two great reformers.

"In Spain one great reformer was born. He was born at Calaroga in Old Castile. There the coat of arms is quartered. On one side a lion is above a castle. On the other side a castle is above a lion, and so one lion is subject and one lion is sovereign.

"This great reformer is God's holy athlete. He was kind to friends but not to enemies. His mind was and is powerful and extraordinary. His mind made his mother dream when she was pregnant with him. Saint Dominic's mother dreamed that she would give birth to a dog — a black-and-white dog that held a flaming torch in its mouth. This dream was a prophecy. Dominicans are called *Domini canes*, or the hounds of the Lord. Black and white are the colors of the Dominican habit — the clothing worn by the Dominicans. The flaming torch is a symbol of the zeal of the Dominican order.

"Francis of Assisi wed Lady Poverty. Saint Dominic also had a wedding; he was wedded to Christian Faith when he was baptized. Saint Dominic and Lady Faith pledged mutual salvation to each other. Because of his baptism, Saint Dominic was saved from original sin, and he devoted his life to saving Lady Faith from heresy. When he was baptized, his godmother answered for him. She had had a dream: She had dreamed that Dominic had a star on his forehead. This dream was prophetic: The star meant that Dominic would have great intelligence, and it meant that he would be a guide for Humankind just like the North Star is a guide for travelers.

"Dominic's name reveals what he is, and it was chosen for that reason. His name means 'belonging to the Lord.' In my opinion, he was chosen specially by Christ to be His aide in the Church's garden.

"From early childhood he made it known that he was a servant of Christ. He also made it known that he loved the first counsel given by Jesus: 'Blessed are the poor in spirit.' He showed his love of voluntary poverty early. Often, his nurse would find that he had crawled out of bed and was sleeping on the floor.

"His father was well named: Felix means 'happy.' His mother was well named: Giovanna means 'grace of God.' Not everyone is well named. Some people who study so they can bear the names of Doctor or Ecclesiastical Lawyer do so because they want worldly gain — not because they want eternal gain.

"He became a remarkable theologian. Figuratively, he inspected the vineyards to make sure that the vines did not wither.

"He requested something from the Pope. At one time, Popes treated the deserving poor well, but now, in 1300, Pope Boniface VIII is corrupt.

"Saint Dominic had to plead for a long time to the Pope of his day for what he wanted. He did not want money. He did not want to disburse the Church's money and keep two or three out of six coins for himself. He did not want a benefice. He did not want to keep the tithes that should go to help the poor. He did want to combat heresy. He did want to spread the good ideas of the souls who now surround you.

"With the permission of the Pope, he used his learning and his strong will to combat heresy. He was like a mighty torrent cleaning evil out of its path and then sending streams to water the good fields."

Beatrice thought, *Saint Dominic battled the Albigensian heresy. The Albigensians denied the Resurrection. He worked for years to persuade the Albigensians to stop believing in heresy and instead to believe in correct doctrine.*

The saved soul continued, "He was one wheel of the two-wheeled Chariot that is the Church. He was excellent, and so is the other wheel of the Chariot — the wheel whom Thomas Aquinas told you about.

"Saint Francis formed his order in 1209, but the Franciscans have declined. At one time the order was like good wine, but now it is like bad wine. Now one sees mold in the wine barrel instead of the crust that good wine leaves.

"At one time the Franciscans walked confidently forward in the footsteps of Saint Francis, but now they have turned around and they are walking backwards, obliterating his footsteps by putting their heels on his toe.

"Soon the harvest time will arrive, and tares will be found and they will not be taken to the storehouse that is Paradise.

"Search through the order of Franciscans. You may find one who is what a Franciscan should be, but most are not. Certainly those who come from Acquasparta or from Casal are not."

Beatrice thought, *Franciscan friars from Acquasparta want to relax the rules of the Franciscan order too much. Matthew of Acquasparta relaxed the rules so much that abuses arose. Ubertino of Casal harshly kept the rules. A Golden Mean is needed. The rules should be neither too lax nor too harsh. Having too lax an enforcement of too few rules is wrong. Matthew of Acquasparta made this mistake. Having too rigid an enforcement of too many rules is wrong. Ubertino of Casal made this mistake.*

A later age will know Mother Teresa. When Mother Teresa founded her order of nuns, the Missionaries of Charity, she at first wanted them to eat only what the poor ate: bread and salt. However, she soon realized that that was too strict. To do good work among the poor, her nuns needed to eat more than bread and salt. However, Mother Teresa was careful not to relax the rules too much. Sometimes, in some places, she thought that her nuns were living too luxuriously, so she got rid of some of the luxuries.

The saved soul continued, "I am Bonaventure. I always put spiritual concerns, not temporal concerns, first."

Beatrice thought, *Saint Bonaventure was born in Tuscony in 1221, but he was named John. He received his new name when he became ill, then recovered. Saint Francis heard of John's remarkable recovery, and he exclaimed, "O buona ventura," which means, "O good fortune." Saint Bonaventure became the superior of the Franciscan friars, and he died in 1274. This is the same year that Thomas Aquinas died.*

Just as Thomas Aquinas, a Dominican, tells the story of Saint Francis, so Saint Bonaventure, a Franciscan, tells the story of Saint Dominic. This is a way of showing respect for a great founder who did not found one's own order.

Again, we see that the Franciscans and the Dominicans in Paradise are not jealous of or competitive in a bad way with each other. They know that they are on the same side.

Saint Bonaventure continued, "Here in this wheel with me are Illuminato and Augustine, both of whom wore the cord that Franciscan friars wear."

Beatrice thought, *Illuminato is an early Italian Franciscan who joined Saint Francis in 1210. Augustine is another early Italian Franciscan who joined Saint Francis in 1210. Augustine was from Assisi, like Saint Francis.*

Saint Bonaventure continued, "Here is Hugh of Saint Victor."

Beatrice thought, *Hugh of the Abbey of Saint Victor near Paris lived in the 12th century. He was an influential mystic and theologian whose students Richard of Saint Victor and Peter Lombard are also known as sages.*

Saint Bonaventure continued, "Here is Peter Mangiador."

Beatrice thought, *Peter Mangiador was known as Petrus Comestor, or Peter the Eater, because he metaphorically consumed books. He was born in French Troyes. In 1147, he became Dean of the Cathedral in Troyes, and later he became Chancellor of the University of Paris.*

Saint Bonaventure continued, "Here is Peter the Spaniard, who wrote 12 books that Humankind studies on Earth."

Beatrice thought, *Peter the Spaniard was actually from Lisbon, Portugal. He was the only Portuguese Pope: Pope John XXI. He served less than a year as Pope. The falling ceiling of a cell killed him; the cell had been hastily built so that he could continue his scholarly pursuits there. He wrote a 12-part book on logic that was widely used.*

Saint Bonaventure continued, "Here is Nathan the prophet."

Beatrice thought, *This Hebrew prophet spoke truth to power and criticized King David for arranging the death of Bathsheba's husband. Nathan appeared before David and said, "There were two men in one city; the one was rich, and the other poor. The rich man had very many flocks and herds, but the poor man had nothing, save one little ewe lamb, which he had bought and nourished. The lamb grew up together with him, and with his children; it ate the food he gave it and drank the drink he gave it, and it lay in his lap, and it was like a child to him. A traveler appeared before the rich man, and the rich man provided food for the traveler, but the rich man did not butcher any of his own flock or of his own herd to provide meat for the traveler. Instead, the rich man took the lamb that belonged to the poor man and butchered it."*

Hearing the story, David was angry and said, "As the Lord lives, the man who has done this thing shall surely die, and he shall restore the lamb fourfold, because he did this thing, and because he had no pity." Nathan said to David, "You are the man. The Lord God of Israel said, 'I anointed you King over Israel, and I delivered you out of the hand of Saul. And I gave you your master's house, and your master's wives to your bosom, and gave you the house of Israel and of Judah; and if that had been too little, I would moreover have given to you much more. Why have you despised the commandment of the Lord, to do evil in his sight? You have killed Uriah the Hittite with the sword, and have taken his wife to be your wife, and have slain him with the sword of the children of Ammon."'

David was the rich man, and Uriah the Hittite was the poor man. To his credit, David repented.

Saint Bonaventure continued, "This is Chrysostom."

Beatrice thought, *Saint John Chrysostom, who died in 407 C.E., was a famed preacher who was called the "golden-mouthed" patriarch of Constantinople; he was noted for his honesty, self-denial, and preaching. He spent time in exile.*

Saint Bonaventure continued, "This is Anselm."

Beatrice thought, *Saint Anselm lived from 1033-1109 C.E. He was an Italian archbishop of Canterbury, and he made the famous ontological argument for God's existence.*

Saint Bonaventure continued, "This is Donatus, who studied the first art."

Beatrice thought, *Donatus was the 4th-century C.E. Roman author of a famous Latin grammar. Grammar is the first art of the seven liberal arts.*

Saint Bonaventure continued, "This is Rabanus."

Beatrice thought, *Rabanus was abbot and archbishop of his native Mainz from 847 to 856 C.E. Like many of the other sages in this circle, he was a great scholar.*

Saint Bonaventure continued, "At my side is the Calabrian Abbot Joachim, a prophet."

Beatrice thought, *Thomas Aquinas has his in-the-living-world adversary Siger of Brabant on his left, and Saint Bonaventure has his in-the-living-world adversary the Abbot Joachim of Flora on his left. The Abbot Joachim of Flora was a Cistercian monk who predicted an approaching final age of history, which he believed would be the age of the everlasting gospel. Saint Bonaventure strove to combat this belief. Once again, we see that two scholars who were rivals on Earth are side by side in Paradise. Once again, we learn that two people of good will can disagree over what is to be regarded as truth. Once again, we see two people of good will who strove to know the truth on Earth. We see that two people of good will can both be sincere seekers after truth even if they arrive at different conclusions.*

Saint Bonaventure continued, "Thomas Aquinas praised Saint Francis, and in his spirit I have praised Saint Dominic. Thomas Aquinas' glowing words moved this wheel of souls to appear here."

Beatrice thought, *Both Saint Francis and Saint Dominic wanted the Church to be healthy, but they emphasized different things.*

Saint Francis emphasized repentance and coming back to God. Christianity, according to Saint Francis, involves more than simply attending church on Sunday morning. Saint Francis emphasized making Christianity a part of your life. Saint Francis emphasized experiencing Christ rather than simply reading the Bible.

Saint Dominic emphasized thinking correctly about God. You must believe the correct doctrine, not an incorrect doctrine that will lead you astray. Saint Dominic wanted preachers to preach the right things.

Of course, both Saint Francis and Saint Dominic are correct. We need repentance. We also need correct doctrine. Without both of those, we can be led astray. Without both of those, we can go wrong.

A healthy Church must emphasize each of these things: repentance and correct doctrine. The Church needed to be reformed, and Saint Francis and Saint Dominic emphasized two things that would make the Church strong.

Chapter 13: Sun — Saint Thomas Aquinas Discusses Solomon

To imagine what Dante saw next, think of the 15 brightest stars in the night sky. Now think of the seven stars that make up the Big Dipper. That makes 22 stars. Add to them the two bright stars of the Little Dipper's mouth for a total of 24 stars, matching the total of 24 bright souls who formed two constellations around Dante and Beatrice. Imagine that the 24 stars form two moving circles around Dante and Beatrice. That will give you some idea of what Dante and Beatrice were seeing.

The two circles of souls whirled and danced, and this sight outstripped a living person's ability to understand in the same way that the fast-moving Primum Mobile outraces the sluggish stream of the Chiana River as it flows through swamps.

Beatrice thought, *In a later age, the Chiana River will flow much faster because the swamplands will have been drained. Of course, the Primum Mobile will still be much, much faster.*

As the souls moved and danced, they sang. They did not sing a hymn to Bacchus. They did not sing a song to Apollo. They sang of the three natures in a triune God, and they sang of the two natures of a Jesus Who was fully human and fully divine.

When the souls had finished their dance and their song, they, rejoicing, turned to Dante and Beatrice.

Thomas Aquinas said, "Two things perplexed you. One, I said, 'Saint Dominic led me and many others along a path where all may be fed if they do not stray from the path.' This I have explained to you. And two, I said, 'A second person has never arisen with as much wisdom as Solomon had.' This still perplexes you. Let me explain what I meant.

"You know that God directly created Adam, from whose rib Eve was created. Eve was lovely, but she sinned, and she tempted Adam to sin.

"You also know that Jesus became fully human in order to save Humankind. That happened as a direct creation of God. Jesus saved Humankind by being crucified and by being wounded with a lance. Jesus paid the price for the past, present, and future sins of Humankind.

"You know that God's light shone brightest in Adam, the first man, and in Jesus Christ.

"And so you are wondering what I meant when I said that no one has ever arisen with as much wisdom as Solomon had.

"Listen carefully. Both you and I believe correctly. What you believe and what I believe are not contradictory.

"Jesus is never parted from the Father or from the Holy Spirit, Who is Love. All creation reflects God. God both created all things and keeps all things in existence as long as they exist. In each moment, God is engaged in the act of creation. If God were to stop His act of creation, all of the universe, including space and time, would go out of existence. God's glory is seen in the entire universe. In some places His glory can be seen more clearly. In some places His glory can be seen less clearly.

"Creation can be direct, or it can be indirect. When God works through nature, which He created, and through the laws of nature, which He also created, the creation is indirect. The creation is also contingent. It can go out of existence. In our everyday existence, we see things go in existence and we see things go out of existence. Things are born, and they die.

"Indirect creation is not as good as direct creation. Human souls are direct creations of God and do not go out of existence. Human bodies are indirect creations of God (using the physical laws of nature, which He created) and human bodies can and do die and go out of existence (although they will be resurrected on the Day of Judgment).

"What is indirectly created is inferior to what is directly created. When God acts directly, as when he created Adam and as when Christ acquired His human nature, the result is perfect. Love (Holy Spirit) and Vision (God's Son) and Power (God the Father) work together to infuse spirit into matter, and the result is perfect. Therefore, the wisdom of Adam and of Jesus was and is perfect. The same is true of Angels. Human wisdom in the material world can never be as perfect as the wisdom of Adam.

"Of course, now you need an explanation of why I stated that a second person has never arisen with as much wisdom as Solomon had.

"To understand what I meant, consider the context of the historical situation. Ask yourself, Who was Solomon? Ask yourself, What did Solomon ask for when God said to him, 'Ask for whatever you want'?

"Of course, Solomon was a king, and he asked God for the wisdom that would make him a good king.

"Solomon did not ask for theological wisdom so that he could answer this question: How many Angels exist?

"Solomon did not ask for logical wisdom so that he could answer this question: Can an absolute premise together with a contingent premise yield an absolute conclusion?

"Solomon did not ask for scientific and philosophic wisdom so that he could answer these questions: Is there a First Mover? Can a motion exist without a cause?

"Solomon did not ask for mathematical wisdom so that he could answer this question: Can a triangle without a right angle using the semicircle's diameter as a base be made to fit in a semicircle?

"What did Solomon ask for? He asked for the practical wisdom that would enable him to be a good and a wise king. Solomon was without equal in the particular gift of wisdom that he received from God. Solomon asked for wisdom to rule well as a king, and he received it.

"In addition, I said that a second person has never *arisen* with as much wisdom as Solomon had. Adam and Jesus did not arise in the sense that Solomon and other human beings arise. Solomon and other human beings arose from the physical matter of the universe in conjunction with the laws of nature that govern matter and energy. God directly created Adam and Jesus.

"Solomon was the wisest of all Kings. Unfortunately, few Kings are good Kings.

"Be wary when you make judgments. Wisdom is difficult to acquire. You can see this in your perplexity when I stated that a second person has never arisen with as much wisdom as Solomon had.

"Fools make judgments quickly. Fools do not consider the evidence.

"Judgments quickly made without evidence are often wrong, and human beings can be so proud that they will not correct a wrong judgment that they have made.

"Sometimes, human beings try to make judgments that they are not ready to make. The ancient Greek philosopher Parmenides believed that the Moon is the source of all things and that all things return to the Moon. His disciple Melissus believed that no motion exists — only the appearance of motion.

Bryson of Heraclea, another Greek philosopher, tried to square the circle —
something that is impossible.

"Errors of judgment in theology, aka heresies, also occur. Sabellius denied
the doctrine of the trinity. He believed that the terms 'Father,' 'Son,' and 'Holy
Ghost' were simply different names for the same single God. Arius believed
that Jesus was created after the Father and was inferior to the Father. Arius
created the Arian heresy.

"No one should trust his or her judgment too quickly.

"Do not be like a farmer who counts his ears of corn before he has harvested
them.

"After all, a brier can be prickly for months and then produce a rose.

"And a ship can safely cross the sea and safely return to outside its harbor
and then sink in the harbor.

"People should not think themselves so wise that when they see one human
being steal and another human being donate money to charity that they know
who will end up in Paradise and who will end up in the Inferno. A once-bad
person can repent at or near the end of life. A once-good person can sin and
not repent at or near the end of life."

Beatrice thought, *When we judge a life, we need to judge an entire life. An
evil man can repent at the last minute, just as a brier can eventually produce a rose.
A good person can become evil at the end of his life, just as a ship that has made
a long voyage can end up sinking back home in its own harbor. Aristotle said that
in order to determine whether a man was happy, we need to look at the whole of
that man's life. After he has died, we will be able to tell if he was happy. God sees
the whole picture — we don't. God knows the end of a person's life and whether or
not they repented. Chances are, most or all people will be surprised by some of those
who make it to Paradise, and by some of those who end up in the Inferno.*

Chapter 14: Sun — Solomon; Mars — Symbolic Cross

When Thomas Aquinas spoke in his circle of souls, words rippled inward to the center, where Dante and Beatrice stood. Now Beatrice spoke, and words rippled outward to the circles of souls.

Beatrice was such a good guide and such a good teacher that she anticipated the questions that Dante would have even before he formulated them in his mind.

Beatrice said to the two circles of souls, "This man has another question, although he has not formulated it yet in his mind and therefore cannot ask it. He needs to know about the radiance that clothes you.

"Will you souls retain your brilliant light eternally?

"If you will retain your brilliance, then when you are reunited with your bodies at the Day of Judgment and begin again to see with your eyes, how will your eyes be able to withstand such brilliance of your own body and of the bodies of other souls?"

Joy can make dancers dance more quickly and can make singers raise their voices. Much like that, the souls in the circle showed their increased happiness in their dance and in their song. They were happy to be able to enlighten Dante.

People on Earth are afraid of dying. If they are right with God, they ought not to be afraid of dying. If they could witness the joy that awaits saved souls in Paradise, they would no longer regret the fact that they must one day die.

The souls sang of the Three that make One: the Father, the Son, and the Holy Ghost that make one omnipotent, omniscient, omnibenevolent God. This God is enclosed by nothing; instead, it encloses everything.

The souls sang the song three times, and this beautiful song is one of the rewards of Paradise.

Then the brightest of the stars in the circle of Thomas Aquinas — the star that is Solomon — began to speak. Although Solomon's star is the brightest, he spoke with a modest tone: "We will wear this brilliance as long as Paradise lasts: forever. Our love, our *caritas*, gives us this brilliance, and our brilliance is in proportion to the amount of love we have and are capable of experiencing.

"On the Day of Judgment, we will be reunited with our bodies, and then we will be more complete and more perfect and therefore more pleasing to ourselves and to God. Our brilliance will increase.

"Our vision of God will increase. We will be able to see more clearly, and we will be able to love even more. Our radiance comes from our love of God.

"Our bodies, which have long been buried, will be even brighter than the brilliance that clothes us now.

"This new brilliance will not be hard to bear. God will strengthen our eyes so that we are able to withstand the radiance of each other. God wants us to be able to bear all that will give us joy."

The souls in the two circles cried, "Amen!" Clearly, they looked forward to being reunited with their bodies, and they looked forward to mothers, fathers, and other loved ones to also get their bodies back. Those things — including bodies — that made you and your loved ones distinctive on Earth are not taken away in Paradise.

And now a third ring of lights appeared. These lights encircled the other two rings of lights, and they glowed as brightly as all those other lights. Dante's eyes were overwhelmed.

Beatrice smiled at Dante, and he was able to raise his eyes again. He saw that Beatrice and he had ascended to another Sphere. This Sphere glowed red, and Dante made a silent prayer of thanks and devotion and gratitude. Dante knew that his prayer was accepted.

Dante and Beatrice were in the Fifth Sphere, which is that of Mars. In the Sphere that was Mars appeared two rays of light of such brilliance that Dante cried out, "O Helios, who adorns the sky!" Helios is both the Sun and a symbol of God.

The two rays of light formed a Cross. The Symbolic Cross is the Cross of the Crusaders. It is a Greek Cross — the two parts that make up the Cross are of equal length. The Symbolic Cross was made up of the saved souls who are associated with Mars, which is the planet that we associate with courage and especially with courage during times of war.

Within the Symbolic Cross, Dante saw an image of Christ.

When Dante the Poet tried to write about this later, after returning to Earth, he found himself unable to describe what he had seen. What he remembered defeated his art as a poet. But anyone who reaches Paradise will be able to see the Symbolic Cross and will forgive Dante for what he was not able to write about it.

The lights that made up the Cross moved from arm to arm and from top to base. The lights sparkled, and they were brilliant.

Humankind makes things such as blinds and curtains to keep out the light, but sometimes a streak of light makes its way through shade, and our eyes see specks floating in the air. Some specks move in a straight line. Some specks move in a slanted line. Some specks move swiftly. Some specks move slowly. The specks create a scene that changes constantly. The lights that made up the Cross were like those specks.

Humankind also creates musical instruments such as the viol and the harp. They have many strings, and the notes they make sound sweet.

The souls who made up the Cross sang a song that entranced Dante the Pilgrim so much that he did not even look at Beatrice. He heard a hymn that contains the words "Arise" and "Conquer," but other than that he knew only that the song sang the highest praise.

Dante felt love as he listened to that song. He thought that nothing could be sweeter than that hymn.

But then he thought, *I may be too rash when I think that nothing could be sweeter than that hymn. Since I have reached the planet Mars, I have not yet looked at Beatrice's eyes. As we ascend the Spheres and we grow closer to God, Beatrice and her eyes become more and more beautiful.*

Chapter 15: Mars — Cacciaguida

The love of others — *caritas* — has an opposite: self-serving love. *Caritas* is always magnanimous, and self-serving love always leads to inequity.

These souls who appeared on Mars have the love that loves others, and the music and the song stopped because these souls knew that Dante wanted to ask questions and to learn things.

These souls felt joy in being able to help Dante. Other souls who had self-serving love have lost forever the joy that is felt in Paradise. They traded joy that is eternal for things that bring joy briefly. Souls who had self-serving love mourn forever in the Inferno — as is right.

Sometimes in the night sky a star seems to fall, but it is actually a meteor. Now a light came from the Cross and approached Dante. The light started from one of the arms and then went to the vertical part of the Cross and down it so that it was as close as possible to Dante.

The light was like fire behind a white screen. The white screen was bright, but within it was a brighter light. The saved soul within was brighter than the brilliant light that clothed it.

The light moved quickly — as quickly as Anchises, Aeneas' father, moved to meet Aeneas when Aeneas went to the Land of the Dead.

Beatrice thought, *The story of Aeneas' journey to Elysium, aka the good part of the Land of the Dead, is told in Virgil's* Aeneid. *Aeneas was in exile, and he was discouraged. He needed a reason for going on, and Anchises gave him that reason by showing Aeneas his illustrious descendants. With renewed vigor, Aeneas went to Italy and accomplished his destiny of becoming an important ancestor of the Roman people.*

Similarly, Dante will be in exile, and he will be discouraged. He will need a reason to go on. He will need to find the right way to react to his exile. Now he will have a meeting with an ancestor who can give him a reason to go on.

The saved soul spoke to Dante in Latin, "*O sanguis meus, O superinfusa gratia Dei, sicut tibi, cui bis unquam celi ianua reclusa?*"

Translating the Latin was not a problem for Dante or for Beatrice, both of whom knew that the saved soul had said, "O blood of mine, O grace of God, has the gate of Paradise ever opened twice for anyone as it has for you?"

Beatrice thought, *The words "O sanguis meus" are quoted from Virgil's* Aeneid. *Anchises spoke these words to Aeneas when Aeneas visited Elysium. Aeneas visited Elysium twice: once while alive, and once after he died. But Elysium is not Paradise. Dante is visiting Paradise now, and he will enter Paradise permanently after he has died.*

Dante looked at the saved soul, and then he looked at Beatrice, who was smiling. Dante also smiled, and it seemed to him that he felt the deepest joy that Paradise offers.

Beatrice thought, *I am very happy that Dante is able to meet this soul. He will be very happy when he finds out who this soul is. He will be much more joyful than he is now.*

The saved soul spoke to Dante, but what the saved soul said was too deep for Dante to comprehend. The saved soul was not being deliberately obtuse. The things that the saved soul was saying were not simple, and difficult language had to be used to express them. In Paradise, such language is understood.

Once the saved soul had stated things that were important although they were not understood by Dante, the saved soul said a few words that Dante could understand: "Blessed be You, God, Three Persons in One Being, Who has shown such grace to one of my descendants!"

The saved soul continued, "I have read the Book of Fate, whose words can never change, and I knew that you were coming. Your being here now has made me happy. Thank you, Beatrice, for all that you have done to bring my descendant to me."

Then the saved soul spoke to Dante, "You believe that I know your thoughts because I can see them in the mind of God, which knows everything, including every thought before it is expressed. You are correct. Because you correctly believe that, you do not ask me who I am and you do not ask why I am so happy to see you.

"But even though I know your thoughts and I know your questions, please use your own voice to express your questions confidently and boldly. I want to hear your voice. You already know that I will answer your questions."

Dante turned to Beatrice, and she smiled to let him know that he ought to speak to the saved soul.

Dante said to the saved soul, "All of you who are saved have no imbalance in your faculties. You can find the proper words to say what you want to say. I, however, am still living, and now I cannot find the proper words to say what I want to say. Only with my heart and not with my words can I thank you for your familial welcome to me here. Also, I would like to know, please, the answer to this question: What is your name?"

The saved soul replied, "I am the root of your family tree. You are one of its branches. I have eagerly anticipated your visit here. The man from whom you have received your family name — Alighieri — is on the first ledge of the Mountain of Purgatory. For one hundred years, he has been carrying a heavy stone to purge his sin of pride. This man is the father of your grandfather: He is your Great-Grandfather. He is my son. I am your Great-Great-Grandfather. You should offer prayers in order to reduce the amount of time he spends on the First Ledge.

"Like you, I am from Florence, but the Florence of my day — the early and mid-1100s — was different from the Florence of your day. Florence was much smaller in my day. Its population still fit behind the ancient walls. Its citizens were at peace then. Its people were pure, and they were temperate. The citizens in the Florence of your day engage in destructive factionalism.

"Women did not dress in clothing that was more beautiful than the woman wearing it. Women did not wear necklaces or tiaras or fancy gowns or fancy belts.

"In the Florence of my day, fathers did not need to fear falling into poverty because of the birth of a daughter. The daughter would be married at an age at which she was mature. She would not be married too young. The dowries were reasonable and could be paid. In the Florence of your day, a man with one daughter is impoverished and a man with two daughters is bankrupt.

"The houses in Florence were smaller then, and people actually lived in them. In the Florence of your day, many large houses are empty. Sometimes, the houses are built to display wealth instead of to be lived in. Sometimes, the houses are empty because the owners have lost their money through riotous living and can no longer afford to maintain them. Sometimes, the houses are empty because the owners have been forced into exile.

"In the Florence of my day, Sardanapalus was not regarded as a role model. In the Florence of your day, this depraved King of Assyria is regarded as setting a standard of debauchery that ought to be imitated, especially in the bedroom.

"The Florence of my day had not surpassed Rome. The Florence of your day surpassed Rome in its ascent, and it will surpass Rome in its fall.

"In the Florence of my day, I saw the nobleman Bellincion Berti wearing a simple leather belt with a simple bone clasp. In the Florence of your day, noblemen wear ornamented belts and jeweled clasps.

"In the Florence of my day, I saw Bellincion Berti's wife in public with a face that was free of makeup. In the Florence of your day, women's faces are painted.

"In the Florence of my day, leading citizens Nerli and Vecchio wore plain leather, and their wives worked with a spindle all day. Such is not the case in the Florence of your day.

"In the Florence of my day, the wives were happy. They knew that when they died, they would be buried in Florence. In the Florence of your day, often people are exiled and so when they die they will be buried elsewhere.

"In the Florence of my day, the wives were not alone in bed — their husbands were with them. In the Florence of your day, many wives sleep alone because their husbands are in France, engaging in trade and making money.

"In the Florence of my day, a wife might be tending a baby in a cradle and speaking baby talk. Another wife might tell her children stories as she worked at a spinning wheel. The stories might be about the Trojans or about Rome or, more locally, about Fiesole.

"In the Florence of my day, stories about the luxuriant excesses of the poet and lawyer Lapo Salterello would have amazed and dismayed the citizens, as would have the sharp tongue, extravagance, and sluttishness of Cianghella.

"In the Florence of your day, citizens would be amazed by stories about the goodness of Cincinnatus, who stopped being a farmer in order to lead Roman troops to victory and then relinquished power and became a farmer again. And they would have been amazed by stories about the goodness of Cornelia, the daughter of the hero Scipio Africanus. Cornelia gave birth to Tiberius and Gaius Gracchi, who tried but failed to save the Roman Republic.

"My mother gave birth to me in Florence, a place of serenity and sweetness and citizens who got along with each other, and in Florence, at the ancient Baptistery, I became a Christian, and I was christened Cacciaguida.

"My brothers were Eliseo and Moronto. My wife came from the valley through which the Po runs, and she brought with her the name 'Alighieri': your name.

"I served the Holy Roman Emperor Conrad III so well that he knighted me, and I fought during the Second Crusade. The Saracens cut me down in battle, and because I was a martyr, I immediately entered Paradise."

Chapter 16: Mars — Cacciaguida's Florence

Dante the Poet thought, *Having pride in the noble blood of ancestors is trivial, but I will no longer be amazed that men on Earth take pride in the noble blood of ancestors. After all, on Earth people are weak, and when I was in Paradise, where no one can desire the wrong thing, I gloried in the noble blood of my ancestor Cacciaguida!*

But there is a right way and a wrong way to have pride of family. A wrong way to have pride of family is to think that having special ancestors makes you special. It doesn't. When your ancestors do something special, they deserve credit for doing that special thing. You do not deserve credit for doing something special unless in fact you do something special.

A right way to have pride of family is when you regard good ancestors as being role models to emulate. If you have an ancestor who did something especially good, and you try to emulate that ancestor, that is a good thing. Having ancestors like that is valuable because they show that it is possible to do something especially good.

Of course, having an especially good ancestor does not mean that you get a Get-Out-of-Hell-Free card. It doesn't work that way. You still have to sincerely repent your sins and try to do good things with your life.

Nobility of character is like a coat. The coat will wear out unless it is added to and repaired. Nobility of character needs to be acquired through good thoughts and good actions day by day or it will wear out.

Dante the Pilgrim prepared to speak to Cacciaguida, and he knew that he wanted to be sure to call him "sir," a word that he had not used when speaking to him previously. The word "sir" was used more often in earlier times than it is used now.

Beatrice smiled at Dante. Seeing the smile, Dante knew that she knew that he was feeling pride of family, and he was reminded of the moment when Guinevere first began to sin with Lancelot — seeing them together, the wife of Malehaut coughed deliberately so that they would know that she was seeing their weakness.

Dante said to Cacciaguida, "Sir, you are my ancestor. Sir, you make me confident enough to speak. Sir, you make my heart rise so that I feel that I am more than myself. My soul is joyful, and it rejoices more than I thought would be possible. Please tell me about your ancestors. Who are they? What famous events happened when you were young? Tell me about Florence. What was its size in your day, and who were the highest citizens?"

The light who was Cacciaguida grew brighter with pleasure at being able to answer Dante's questions. The brightness was like that of glowing coals bursting into flames when a breeze blows over the coals.

Cacciaguida grew more beautiful, and with a sweet voice that was more refined than the voices of the Florentines of Dante's day, Cacciaguida said, "From the Annunciation in which the Angel Gabriel told Mary 'Ave' to the day that my mother, who is now a saint in Paradise, gave birth to me, the planet Mars made 580 orbits. In other words, I was born in the year 1091 C.E.

"The house I was born in lies in the path taken by the runners in the annual race that takes place on June 24: the Feast of Saint John. To be exact, I was born at Porta San Piero.

"About my ancestors we need not talk. We need not mention their names or where they came from. I wish to avoid boasting about my ancestors.

"Florence in my day was much smaller than it is now. Two important boundaries of Florence were the statue of Mars on the Ponte Vecchio and the baptistery of St. John. Those Florentines able to bear weapons in my day numbered 6,000, which is about one-fifth of those who are able to bear weapons in the Florence of your day.

"The people who lived in the Florence of my day were actually Florentines. In the Florence of your day, many people who live in Florence originally came from Campi, Certaldo, and Fighine. They brought their small-town, impoverished, backwoods ways into what should be a great city. Florence made a mistake by growing and incorporating these small towns.

"It would be much better for Florence if it were smaller, and its boundaries reached only as far as Galluzzo and Trespiano. That way, Campi, Certaldo, and Fighine would be outside the territory controlled by Florence. If Florence had not grown, then its citizens would not include the yokel who is Baldo d'Aguglione. He is a rip-off artist who stole salt."

Beatrice thought, *Baldo d'Aguglione will be a personal enemy to Dante. After Dante and other Guelfs are banished into exile from Florence, Baldo d'Aguglione will rescind the banishment of many Guelfs and allow them back into Florence, but he will make sure that Dante remains banished from Florence.*

Cacciaguida continued, "If Florence had not grown, then its citizens would also not include Fazio de' Morubaldini of Signa, a lawyer whose more accurate job titles include swindler, barrator, and grafter."

A barrator engages in graft.

Cacciaguida continued, "if only the Pope and the Cardinals had not hated the Holy Roman Emperor so much and had not treated him the way a bad stepmother treats someone she does not consider a son, but had instead treated him the way a good mother treats a good son, then a newly minted Florentine who wheels and deals in your city and whose name I will not mention would be back in Semifonte, the place where his grandfather begged for scraps.

"In addition, if things were right in the world, then Florence would never have bought the castle of Montemurlo from the Counts Guidi. Also, the parish of Acone would still have as citizens the Cerchi, who are White Guelfs in the Florence of your time and who have caused civic disturbances by feuding with the Donati family. And Valdigreve would still have as citizens the family Buondelmonti, who have caused much trouble in Florence.

"Florence followed an aggressive policy of expansion after my day, and it has resulted in a mixed population: some Florentine, and some unassimilated. Food not properly digested is bad for you, and a population not properly digested is bad for Florence.

"A large size need not be a good size. It is better to have a small, well-governed city than a large, badly governed city. The Florence of my day was small but well governed. The Florence of your day is large but badly governed.

"Imagine people with swords. One well-trained swordsman is much more effective than five amateur swordsmen.

"Cities do not always remain healthy. Luni and Urbisaglia and Sinigaglia and Chiusi are either dead or dying and almost extinct.

"Families also do not always remain healthy. A city can die out, and so can a family.

"The works of Humankind — such as a city — must come eventually to an end. To individual human beings, whose life is so short, it may seem as if a city will last forever, but the city will not. And so with families.

"Let me mention some formerly great families who are not great now. They were noble in my day, and they are nonexistent or weak in your day.

"The Wheel of Fortune turns, and its turning affects Florence and the families of Florence.

"I knew many illustrious families: the Ughi, the Catellini, the Greci, the Filippi, the Aberichi, the Ormanni. Even when these families were declining, their members were illustrious. These were good families in the Florence of my day, but the citizens of the Florence of your day do not know them.

"I also knew the families that were both great and old: the dell'Arca, the Sannella, the Soldanieri, the Ardinghi, the Bostichi.

"The good Ravignani family once lived near the Gate at the Porta Dan Piero, which is now controlled by a family who is bringing much destructiveness to Florence. The Ravignani family birthed Guido the Count and the good people bearing the name Bellincione.

"The della Pressa family knew how to govern well in the Florence of my day, and the Galigaio family were noble."

Dante thought, *Both families declined. The della Pressa family, who were Ghibellines, betrayed Florence at Montaperti. In 1260, five years before I was born, the Ghibellines fought the Guelfs in the Battle of Montaperti. The Ghibellines defeated the Guelfs and stained the Arbia River red with Guelf blood. In the Florence of my day, the Galigaio family is no longer noble.*

Cacciaguida continued, "In the Florence of my day, the great families included the Galli, the Sacchetti, the Giuochi, the Fifanti, and the Barucci, and the family whose members blush in the Florence of your day because they committed fraud and stole salt.

"Another great family in the Florence of my day was the Calfucci, which is extinct in the Florence of your day but from whom sprang the Donati family. Other great families in the Florence of my day were the Arrigucci and the Sizii.

"These families were great, but they were proud, and pride ruined them. One such proud family was the Lamberti, whose arms bore golden balls against a field of blue. Mosca, who is now in the Inferno, was a member of this family.

"These families have descendants who let livings remain vacant so that they can benefit from the income. Those livings ought to be filled by religious who can help the people.

"In my day, a family that became notorious for greed and cowardice in your day was beginning to rise, although it was of such a lower class that Ubertino Donati was not pleased when his father-in-law married Ubertino's wife's sister to a member of that family. That family is like a dragon to anyone who is weak, and it is like a lamb to anyone who is strong.”

Beatrice thought, *That family includes a person who will take possession of Dante's property when Dante is exiled. That person will oppose Dante's being allowed to return to Florence. After Dante is exiled, he will never again see Florence.*

Cacciaguida continued, “Other families who were notable in my day but have declined in your day include some Ghibelline families: the Caponsacchi, the Guidi, and the Infangati. The della Pera family — incredible! — were once so well known in Florence that a city gate was named after it.

“Hugh of Brandenburg honored six Florentine families by conferring knighthood upon them. All of these families adopted coats of arms that were variants of Hugh's own coat of arms. Giano della Bella, a descendant of one of these families, however, tried to reform the nobles in 1293 and was banished in 1295. All of these great Florentine noble families should support the Holy Roman Emperor.

“In my day the Gualterrotti and the Importuni were great families, but their new neighbors were the Buondelmonti, who created great strife in Florence.

“I wish that the Buondelmonti family had never come to Florence because it is the family whose coming started the factionalism in Florence.

“Buondelmonte of the Buondelmonti family was engaged to be married to a woman of the Amidei family, but he had a chance to make a better marriage to a woman of the Donati family, so he jilted his bride-to-be on the wedding day. This was, of course, a major insult to her and her family, and members of her family murdered Buondelmonte — Mosca instigated the murder. This led to factionalism in Florence, and the split of its citizens into the Guelf and the Ghibelline groups.

“If only Buondelmonte had died by drowning in the Ema River before he came to Florence, Florence and its citizens — and you — would be much better off.

“The first Guelf is Buondelmonte, and the first Ghibelline is his murderer.

“Buondelmonte, who is the founder of your own political party, did the wrong thing by jilting the woman he was engaged to. Of course, the man who murdered him also did the wrong thing. The main point is this: Political factionalism can be a very bad thing.

"Buondelmonte was murdered at the foot of the statue of Mars in Florence on Easter morning in 1215 C.E. — a fitting sacrifice to the god of war because of all the blood that was shed then and in the years following.

"Because of the action of Buondelmonte, a Florence that was peaceful in my own time is now filled with civic strife for no good reason.

"When the good families of my day ruled Florence, I saw only glory and justice.

"I did not see the civic strife of your day. I did not see the wars between the Guelfs and the Ghibellines. I did not see the Ghibelline standard of a white lily against a red field. I did not see the Guelf standard of a red lily against a white field. I did not see the victor drag the standard of the loser in the dust. I did not see the civic strife that plagues the Florence of your day."

Chapter 17: Mars — Cacciaguida's Prophecy

Phaëthon had heard rumors that he was the son of Apollo, and he went to Apollo to see if the rumors were true. Apollo assured him that the rumors were true, but Phaëthon demanded that his father allow him to drive the chariot of the Sun to prove that he was his father. Apollo allowed him to do this, but the result was disastrous: Phaëthon could not control the horses that pulled the chariot, and Jupiter killed him so that he would not burn up the Earth. For that reason, fathers are wary in granting what their sons request.

Like Phaëthon, Dante wanted to know whether the vague things he had heard were true, and if so, he wanted to try to get some benefit from having that knowledge. Dante felt that he was with the two people — Beatrice and his ancestor Cacciaguida — who would be best able to enlighten him.

Beatrice knew what Dante was thinking, and she knew that Dante ought to know about his upcoming exile, but she felt that it would be better that Dante's ancestor Cacciaguida tell him and so she said to Dante, "I know that you have questions burning inside you. Go ahead and ask them. Of course, we already know what your questions are, but you should learn to ask for what you want: This is a skill that will be necessary for your future survival."

Dante said to Cacciaguida, "Cherished ancestor in Paradise, you have special knowledge. Human beings in the living world have some knowledge. We know that a triangle cannot contain two obtuse angles. A triangle has three angles that add up to exactly 180 degrees. An obtuse angle has more than 90 degrees, so two obtuse angles equal more than 180 degrees, and so whatever geometric figure is formed will not be a triangle.

"As clearly as human beings in the living world know that, so clearly do you know the past, the present, and the future because you can see into the mind of God. Whatever contingent being — a being that is capable of existing and of not existing, although not at the same time — will come into existence, you know that it will come into existence before it comes into existence. Contingent existence is different from necessary existence, which has always existed and always will exist. God has necessary existence.

"While I was still with Virgil and was climbing the Mountain of Purgatory and descending the circles of the Inferno, many souls made vague but ominous statements about my future life."

Beatrice thought, *During his journey throughout the Inferno and the Mountain of Purgatory, Dante has heard hints of his future exile.*

In the Inferno, Ciacco prophesied to Dante, "After much more fighting, one party will drive out the other party. Then within three years the positions will be reversed, and the party that was victorious will be defeated, and the party that was defeated will be victorious."

In the Inferno, Farinata revealed that Dante will soon be sent into exile — within 50 months.

In the Inferno, Brunetto Latini prophesied hard times for Dante. Brunetto's prophecy stated that both political parties will regard Dante as an enemy.

In the Inferno, Vanni Fucci predicted coming trouble for Dante and for Florence. Vanni told Dante of the coming troubles, including the expulsion of the White Guelfs from Florence by the Black Guelfs, and he added that he was telling Dante this bad news so that Dante would suffer.

On the Mountain of Purgatory, Dante talked with Conrad Malaspina, who made a prediction: Within seven years Dante will have need of the generosity of the Malaspina family.

On the Mountain of Purgatory, Oderisi of Gubbio prophesied that Dante will learn the humiliation of begging.

On the Mountain of Purgatory, the poet Bonagiunta Da Lucca prophesied that a woman from his city, which is reviled, will make Dante praise his city.

Dante continued, "Because of these prophecies, I am better prepared to withstand bad fortune. I would like to know in more detail what bad fortune is coming. If I know what bad fortune will happen to me, I may be able to blunt its force."

Dante had done as Beatrice had wished, and now Cacciaguida answered him. His reply was not vague, like the ancient, tricky oracles whose words can mean more than one thing.

Oracles that existed before Christ's crucifixion could be misleading, and they could lead people astray. Some prophecies were deliberately ambiguous. For example, Croesus, the King of Lydia, was thinking about attacking Persia. He sent an emissary to the Delphic Oracle to ask whether he should do that.

The Delphic Oracle responded that if he attacked Persia, "A mighty empire will fall." Croesus regarded the oracle as propitious, and he attacked Persia. A mighty empire did fall; unfortunately, the mighty empire that fell was his own empire.

Cacciaguida replied to Dante with clear, easily understandable words. Cacciaguida was happy to enlighten Dante.

Cacciaguida said to Dante, "God knows all about the existence and the nonexistence of all contingent things. God knows the past, the present, and the future. But this does not take away from free will. God exists outside of space and time, and God sees the past, the present, and the future all at the same time. God sees human beings use their free will either for good or for ill. A human being may watch a boat going down a stream. Watching the boat does not mean that the human being is controlling the actions of the boat.

"From the vision that the mind of God has, I can see what will happen to you in the future.

"Hippolytus' stepmother fell in love with him and tried to seduce him. Hippolytus resisted, and his stepmother lied and said that Hippolytus had tried to force himself on her. Therefore, Hippolytus, although innocent, was banished from his city: Athens.

"You, also, although innocent, will be banished from your city: Florence. You will be exiled. A Pope who each day engages in simony and sells Christ is now planning the events that will lead to your exile.

"As is usual, the public will blame the one who is innocent and will praise the one who is guilty. And yet, in the long run, the truth shall be known.

"You will have to leave Florence and everything that is valuable to you. You will have to leave behind your family. This is the first of the evils that await you.

"You will learn how salty the bread of other people is, and you will learn to walk down steps that belong to other people and to walk up steps that belong to other people."

Beatrice thought, *Dante will have to eat different kinds of food than what he is used to getting in Florence. Dante will be in unfamiliar places. He will eat the food of other people, and he will stay at the homes of other people. Of course, when he does that, he is not at home. He is not in control. To an extent, he will have to do what other people want him to do.*

In addition, people in Florence do not put salt in their bread, and so when they travel outside of Florence and eat bread, they notice how salty the bread is.

Bread is important. The Bible calls bread the staff of life. Bread is also an important part of the Eucharist — a Christian sacrament in which bread represents the body of Christ and wine represents the blood of Christ.

Cacciaguida continued, "What will be worse will be the company you fall in with. The people you will be around will be despicable and senseless."

Beatrice thought, *By 1300, the Guelfs had defeated the Ghibellines in Florence. However, the Guelfs divided into two factions: the White Guelfs and the Black Guelfs. The White Guelfs will throw the Black Guelfs out of Florence. Corso Donati will persuade Pope Boniface VIII to send Charles of Valois and his troops to Florence. Charles of Valois, working with Pope Boniface VIII, will pretend to be a peacekeeper, but actually he will be working to have the Black Guelfs take control of Florence and expel the White Guelfs. This will happen while Dante, a White Guelf, is away from Florence in the fall of 1301. On 1 November 1301, Charles of Valois will enter Florence and give control of the city to the Black Guelfs. Cante de' Gabrielli will issue a proclamation on 27 January 1302 that will falsely charge Dante with barratry and will give him three days to return to Florence to reply to the charges and to pay a huge fine. Dante wisely will stay away from Florence. On 10 March 1302, Cante de' Gabrielli will issue another proclamation that will condemn Dante to be burned to death if he ever returns to Florence. The reason for the death sentence will be that Dante failed to show up to reply to the charges against him.*

For a while after he is exiled, Dante will think that he will return to Florence in a few weeks, but that will not happen. For a while after he is exiled, Dante will plot with other White Guelfs about how they can return to Florence. Their plots will fail. Dante will never return to Florence after he is exiled.

Cacciaguida continued, "The company you fall in with will turn against you and hate you. They will be ungrateful, but history and their own deeds will show that they, not you, are in the wrong.

"Instead of being in a party with others, you will gain honor by being in a party of one: yourself."

Beatrice thought, *One thing that Dante has been learning during his journey through the afterlife is to avoid extreme factionalism. The people he will meet with after his exile will turn out to be extreme factionalists of the type that Farinata was in the Inferno.*

Eventually, Dante will do the right thing and become a party of one. He will rightfully criticize both the White Guelfs and the Black Guelfs, and he will rightly criticize both the Guelfs and the Ghibellines.

After his exile, Dante will be tempted to work very hard to get back into Florence. One way to do that is to raise an army and go to war. Of course, if you do that, lots of people will die, and lots of people will be hurt. Soldiers will die, and their families will be without breadwinners.

Eventually, Dante will stop plotting with other people about how to get back into Florence. He will stop engaging in bad factionalism. He will learn that other things are important. We should not say, "My political party, right or wrong."

Farinata is a person who put himself and his political party first, and look where he ended up.

Cacciaguida continued, "You will also meet and enjoy the hospitality of good people. After leaving the bad people, you will find refuge first with the great Lombard, Bartolommeo della Scala of Verona, whose coat of arms shows an eagle and a ladder. He will give you what you need even before you ask for it.

"With him will be his younger brother, Can Grande della Scala, who will win great renown. Right now, in 1300, he is not known because he is only nine years old, but he will quickly make his merit known — even before the Gascon tricks Henry by first supporting him and then withdrawing that support."

Cacciaguida thought, *In 1312, Pope Clement V, aka the Gascon, will trick Holy Roman Emperor Henry VII.*

Cacciaguida continued, "Can Grande della Scala will scorn the pursuit of wealth and will not be afraid to work. His generosity will be so widely known that even his enemies will acknowledge it.

"Look at him and expect great things from him. Because of him, many deserving beggars will be raised high and many undeserving wealthy men will be brought low."

Cacciaguida then told Dante about some of the things that Can Grande della Scala would accomplish, but he forbade him to talk or write about them.

Then Cacciaguida continued, "You see your future. You know the snares that lie ahead. Do not envy Corso Donati or Pope Boniface VIII. Your future is brighter than their futures despite the pain that they will inflict on you."

Cacciaguida had answered Dante's question, and Dante was able to add what he had learned to the web of knowledge that he had already acquired.

Dante sought reassurance and advice from his virtuous ancestor who knew the future and loved him: "Father, I see the hardships that lie ahead of me — hardships that do much damage to those who are unprepared.

"I know that I will not be able to live in Florence, the place I hold most dear. I do not want to lose the ability to live elsewhere because of what I can write.

"I have traveled down the Inferno and up the Mountain of Purgatory and from heavenly Sphere to heavenly Sphere with the help of Beatrice, and I have learned much. If I write the truth about what I have learned, I will make enemies.

"And yet, if I do not write the truth about what I have learned, what I write will not last. People of the future will not read what I write."

Beatrice thought, *Dante will be able to bring good out of exile. He will be exiled from Florence, but he will be able to learn from the experience, and he will be able to pass on what he learns to other people when he writes his* Divine Comedy.

Dante will be like an Old Testament prophet who speaks truth to power. His exile will become a kind of pilgrimage.

In doing this, Dante will make many, many people very, very angry at him. Many, many powerful people will appear in the Inferno *part of his* Divine Comedy. *Their families will still be alive.*

Dante will be in exile, which means that he won't have much to lose. Because he won't have much to lose, he will have a certain amount of freedom. Not having much to lose means that he can tell the truth. What will someone do if they become angry at him: exile him? He will be already in exile.

Dante is worried. If he is going to tell his story, he has to tell it the right way if his message will endure.

Brunetto Latini wrote for the wrong reasons. He wanted to become famous, and so he wrote to become famous. It worked, but not for long. Brunetto Latini was well known when he was alive, but unless Dante puts him in the Inferno *Brunetto Latini will be forgotten.*

What Dante needs to do is to tell the truth. The Old Testament prophets are remembered because they told the truth. Dante knows that it will take courage to tell the truth. In order to be remembered, Dante must tell the truth, even though the truth will make other people angry.

Dante will make the right choice and write the truth about what he has learned. People 700 years from now will read what he writes — and people 700 years after that will read what he writes.

Cacciaguida's light grew brighter because he was joyful at being able to give Dante advice that was exactly right.

Cacciaguida said, "Some people have dark consciences, and yes, they will be angry at what you write. But do not lie. Tell the truth. Everything you have learned, write. If some people are wounded by what you write, let them bind their wounds.

"What you write may seem bitter at first, but it will be good medicine. Although some people will sting from the words; nevertheless, the words will be beneficial to them.

"Your words will hit hard at bad Popes and bad politicians, but these are the people who most need to read what you write.

"During your journey through the afterlife, you have met and seen many prominent people. Use them in what you write. Readers will pay attention to what you write if you write about prominent people. Readers will know about the prominent people, and they will know that you are writing the truth. They will learn from these examples. Use clear examples, and make clear arguments."

Beatrice thought, *Dante will engage in much criticism in* The Divine Comedy, *but his purpose will be ultimately creative rather than destructive. If a building is a wreck, tear it down and then build another one in its place. If you have bad habits, get rid of the bad habits so that you can substitute good habits in their place. If the Church needs to be reformed, criticize it so that it can be reformed and become both better and stronger.*

Dante's words will be hard to hear, but they can provide much-needed nourishment.

Cacciaguida was a Crusader with a sword, and he has let Dante know that he must be a Crusader with a pen.

Chapter 18: Jupiter — Lovers of Justice

Cacciaguida was happy because he knew that Dante would eventually write *The Divine Comedy*.

Dante was silent for a while as he thought about the exile that awaited him.

Beatrice said to Dante, "Think about other things than the bad things. Think about Paradise, where I dwell with God, Who is able to lift the weight of every insult and every bad thing."

Dante turned and faced Beatrice. Her eyes were beautiful, and they were filled with love. They were filled with more love than can be experienced on Earth — that amount of love is reserved for Paradise. For Dante to be able to experience so much love on Earth, he would need divine help.

But as he looked at the love in Beatrice's eyes, he knew that he longed for nothing except to continue looking into her eyes, through which God's joy was shining.

With a dazzling smile, Beatrice said, "Turn around and listen to Cacciaguida. Paradise can be found in his eyes, too."

Faces and eyes reveal the deepest wishes of a person, and Dante saw that Cacciaguida wished to speak to him.

Cacciaguida said, "Mars is the fifth Sphere. Think of the Spheres as resembling a tree. This tree would get nourishment from the crown, not the roots, because the crown of the tree would be the place where God dwells: the Mystic Empyrean. This tree would always bear fruit in every season, and it would never lose its leaves.

"Here on Mars dwell souls who were so famous on Earth that they would inspire every poet to write better.

"Look up. Look at the horizontal arms of the Cross. I will name some souls, and you will see them flash across the arms as quickly as lightning flashes through a cloud. The naming and the flashing-by will occur simultaneously."

As Cacciaguida pronounced each name, Dante saw a light flashing across the arms of the Cross. In all, Cacciaguida pronounced the names of eight holy warriors.

Joshua flashed across the arms of the Cross. Moses never made it to the Holy Land. Joshua was the successor of Moses, and he was the conqueror of the Holy Land. Joshua conquered Jericho, and he allowed Rahab, the whore of Jericho, and her children to remain alive. Joshua conquered Canaan.

Judas Maccabaeus flashed across the arms of the Cross. Judas Maccabaeus, a Jewish general, fought the Syrians in the 2nd century B.C.E. because King Antiochus of Syria was persecuting the Jews. He restored and purified the temple at Jerusalem, but later the Syrians defeated and killed him. When Dante saw this light flash by, he thought of a child's top that spun and was powered by its own joy.

Charlemagne flashed across the arms of the Cross. Charlemagne was the restorer of the Western Roman Empire. He was the Holy Roman Emperor.

Roland flashed across the arms of the Cross. Roland, Charlemagne's nephew, fought the Saracens, aka Muslims, in Spain. Roland was famous for his ivory horn and the sound it made. He was Charlemagne's paladin.

William of Orange flashed across the arms of the Cross. William of Orange fought the Saracens in southern France, and he was the living ideal of the Christian knight. William of Orange was the hero of the Old French epic titled the *Aliscans*.

Renouard flashed across the arms of the Cross. Renouard was a huge Saracen who converted to Christianity and fought on the side of William of Orange; in addition, he was William's brother-in-law. William found him working as a slave in a royal kitchen and freed him. In late life, they lived as monks in the same monastery.

Duke Godfrey flashed across the arms of the Cross. Duke Godfrey was the leader of the First Crusade. He fought the Saracens in the Holy Land, and he became the first Christian King of Jerusalem. He died in 1100 C.E.

Robert Guiscard flashed across the arms of the Cross. The 11th-century Robert Guiscard fought the Saracens in Sicily and in southern Italy, and he founded the Norman dynasty there. He died in 1085 C.E.

Having recited the names of the holy warriors, Cacciaguida rejoined the other souls who made up the Cross, and he sang.

Dante turned to Beatrice to find out what he should do next, and he saw that she had grown brighter and more beautiful. A human being can do good deeds and take joy in doing good deeds and can realize that he or she has grown more virtuous by doing good deeds. Much like that, seeing that Beatrice had grown brighter, he realized that he was in a Sphere that was further away from Earth and was making a bigger orbit around Earth than Mars had done.

He also noticed that the color in Beatrice's face had changed like a blush leaving the face of a lady. Before, it had been reddish with the glow of Mars and now it was white with the glow of Jupiter, which was named after the Roman god who was the king of gods and of men.

Beatrice thought, *The virtue that is associated with Jupiter is justice, and the souls found here are the souls of the just.*

The souls of the just were lights who moved and formed visible speech. Just like birds rise from the edge of water as if they are celebrating an abundance of food, the souls flew together, sometimes in a group and sometimes in a line.

These souls formed letters: First a D, and then an I, and then an L. They sang while forming a letter, but having formed the letter, they stopped singing and allowed Dante enough time to see and remember the letter, and then the souls sang and formed another letter.

Dante thought, *Please, Muses, help me to remember the letters so that I can show them later to other people.*

He remembered. The souls spelled out this message: *DILIGITE IUSTITIAM QUI IUDICATIS TERRAM.*

Dante thought, *Translated from the Latin, the message means "LOVE JUSTICE, YOU WHO RULE THE EARTH." This is the beginning of the first chapter of the book titled "Wisdom of Solomon": "Love justice, you who rule the Earth: think of the Lord with a good heart, and in the simplicity of your heart seek him."*

The souls had formed in the shape of the final M. The letter was gold, and Jupiter in the background was silver. More souls joined the M, and they sang.

Dante thought that they sang about Ultimate Good — perhaps. He was not able to understand some things in Paradise.

When a fire is stirred, sparks rise up. At one time, people thought — incorrectly — that they could foretell the future by examining these sparks.

The souls — it seemed that there were more than a thousand of them — rose to various heights and formed a new shape: that of an Eagle.

Beatrice thought, *The Eagle is a symbol of Empire, and it is a symbol of justice. Roman law is to be greatly respected.*

Guiding the souls was God, Who also guides birds as they build their nests. God is the Creator, and God needs no one to guide His hand, but He is able to guide others.

Dante the Poet thought, *Justice can be found on Earth, and many souls who had the quality of being just while on Earth are present here. Our idea of Justice comes from Paradise, and we can see Justice more clearly when our eyes are not blinded by greed for money.*

God's wrath is rightfully directed against those who try to turn a temple into a marketplace for buying and for selling. The walls of a temple are built with miracles and martyrs, not with greed for money.

May just souls in Paradise pray for those who are misled on Earth by people who provide bad examples although they should provide good examples.

At one time, warriors fought wars with swords. Now, bad Popes fight wars by excommunicating people and denying them what God the Father would deny to no one. For example, Pope Gregory VII, who died in 1085 C.E., excommunicated Holy Roman Emperor Henry IV twice. A later pope, Pope John XXII, wrote excommunications simply so he could make money by canceling the excommunications.

Excommunication can be used ethically, but to use it for political and monetary purposes is to misuse it.

Popes who use excommunications unethically should remember that Peter and Paul are still alive in Paradise after having died to save the Church.

Popes who use excommunications unethically say, "My heart is set on John the Baptist, who lived alone in the wilderness and who died after Salome danced for Herod and then asked for John the Baptist's head on a platter. I know nothing of Peter the Fisherman or of Paul."

Yes, the heart of these popes is set on John the Baptist. This sounds good at first, but it is actually bad. The image of John the Baptist is stamped on the gold coins of Florence.

Popes who use excommunications unethically are more concerned with collecting gold coins than with doing the will of God. Popes who use excommunications unethically know a lot more about John the Baptist — or rather, John the Baptist's image on gold coins — than they do about Saint Peter or Saint Paul.

Chapter 19: Jupiter — Symbolic Eagle

Before Dante's eyes was the figure of the Eagle, a figure that was formed by the joyful souls of the just.

Each soul of the just was like a ruby through which a ray of the Sun was passing and then striking Dante's eyes.

And what Dante saw was something that no other living person else has ever spoken or written about, or even imagined.

Dante saw the beak of the Eagle move, and the Eagle spoke. The Eagle used the singular — "I" and "Mine" — but because all the souls of the just were speaking as one, it could have used the plural — "We" and "Ours."

The Eagle said, "On Earth I was just and pious, and so I am in Paradise and I am appearing before you on this Sphere. I feel as much glory as it is possible for me to feel. On Earth, the memory of me is such that even evil people praise me although they will not follow my example."

Many burning coals produce one glowing heat, and the many souls of the just produced one voice.

Dante said, "You are like many flowers whose fragrances produce one perfume; please breathe forth more words and satisfy my craving to have my questions about justice answered. You are able to directly see the justice that is within the mind of God.

"You know that I am eager to hear you answer my questions, and you know what my questions are that I have wished for a time to have answered."

A falcon that is freed from the hood covering its eyes will stretch its neck and beat its wings in its eagerness to take flight. The Eagle moved similarly and sang a hymn to God.

The Eagle then said to Dante, "God is the One Who created the universe and marked its limits and brought order out of chaos, but even God cannot create something that has His perfection. All that God creates is less perfect than God.

"This is shown with the first Prideful Power, Lucifer, who, although he was the most beautiful and he was the closest to God, used his free will to rebel against God. Lucifer should have waited for grace from God to ripen his understanding. Instead, Lucifer wanted to immediately become God's equal, and he plunged to Earth green and unripe."

Beatrice thought, *If God's greatest created creature can rebel and fall, then it is possible for all of God's other created creatures to rebel and fall. Any creature who rebels against God lacks understanding.*

The Eagle continued, "Humankind has knowledge, but the knowledge of Humankind is only a small fraction of the knowledge that God has. Although Humankind lacks the knowledge that God has, Humankind does have enough knowledge to know how much knowledge Humankind lacks.

"Humankind cannot comprehend the mind of God any more than it can see the deep bottom of the ocean. Yes, Humankind can see the bottom near the shore, but further out into the ocean, Humankind cannot see the bottom of the ocean. But even though Humankind cannot see it, it still exists.

"Truth and light come from God; all else is falsehood and darkness. The answer you seek is hidden in the mind of God.

"The questions that you want to have answered are these: 'Consider a human being who is born in a country in which no one knows about Christ. No one can speak or write about Him because no one knows Him. This human being, as far as human reason can tell, always acts correctly and always desires correctly. This human being, who has never been baptized, dies. This human being is then denied Paradise. Is it just for this human being to be denied Paradise? Is this human being at fault for never having known Christ?'

"Who are you to condemn God's judgment? It is as if you can barely see beyond your nose and you want to pass judgment on something that happened a thousand miles away!

"Human reason cannot know many things, but fortunately, reason has holy scripture to use as a guide to aid its understanding.

"Humankind needs to remember that God is all-good. What God desires is always just. What God does is always just. If something is in accordance with the will of God, it is just."

Dante thought, *Our finite human minds are simply unable to understand God's infinite mind. We underestimate God's mind if we assume that we can understand the things that God knows. Some things are a mystery. A mystery is something that human reason cannot understand and cannot explain. All we can do is to accept mystery because we cannot explain it. God created Limbo, and He created the rest of the Inferno. We have to assume that He had a good reason for doing this.*

After feeding its young, a stork will fly around the nest, and its chick will raise its head to look at it. Much like that, the Eagle took flight — the souls who made up its wings worked together — and Dante raised his head to look at it.

Circling around Dante, the Eagle sang, "What I sing cannot be understood by human beings on Earth: the harmonics and language are too difficult for them to understand. And so it is with Eternal Judgment."

The souls stopped singing, and then, still in the form of the Eagle, they said as one, "In Paradise, everyone has had faith in Christ, whether they had faith before He was crucified or after.

"But many people who cry 'Christ! Christ!' frequently and loudly on Earth will not be as close to God on the Day of Judgment as will many people who have never heard of Christ.

"Pagans in Ethiopia and elsewhere will condemn such Christians who are Christians in name only."

Dante thought, *Being Christian is enough to get you into Paradise, but just saying that you are Christian is not enough to get you into Paradise. To know this, all you have to do is look into the Inferno and see all the Popes there. Many of the unrepentant sinners in the Inferno said that they were Christian. Guido da Montefeltro attempted to scam God into thinking that he was a Christian, but Guido's scam did not work.*

The Eagle continued, "On the Day of Judgment, souls will be divided into two groups. One group of souls will be rich forever after; the other group of souls will be poor forever after."

Dante thought, *In Matthew 25:31-46, we read about the Day of Judgment:*

31: When the Son of man shall come in His glory, and all the holy Angels with Him, then shall He sit on the throne of His glory:

32: And before Him shall be gathered all nations: and He shall separate them one from another, as a shepherd divides his sheep from the goats,

33: And He shall set the sheep on his right hand, but the goats on the left.

34: Then shall the King say to them on His right hand, "Come, you blessed of My Father, inherit the kingdom prepared for you from the foundation of the world.

35: "For I was hungry, and you gave me food: I was thirsty, and you gave me drink: I was a stranger, and you took me in.

36: *"I was naked, and you clothed me: I was sick, and you visited me: I was in prison, and you came to visit me."*

37: *Then shall the righteous answer Him, saying, "Lord, when saw we You hungry, and fed You, or thirsty, and gave You drink?*

38: *"When did we see You as a stranger, and took You in, or naked, and clothed You?*

39: *"Or when did we see You sick, or in prison, and came to visit You?"*

40: *And the King shall answer and say to them, "Truly I say to you, Inasmuch as you have done it to one of the least of these My brethren, you have done it to Me."*

41: *Then shall He say also to them on the left hand, "Depart from me, you cursed, into everlasting fire, prepared for the devil and his Angels.*

42: *"For I was hungry, and you gave Me no food: I was thirsty, and you gave Me no drink.*

43: *"I was a stranger, and you took Me not in: naked, and you did not clothe Me: sick, and in prison, and you did not visit Me."*

44: *Then shall they also answer him, saying, "Lord, when did we see You hungry, or thirsty, or as a stranger, or naked, or sick, or in prison, and did not minister to You?"*

45: *Then shall He answer them, saying, "Truly I say to you, Inasmuch as you did it not to one of the least of these, you did it not to Me."*

46: *And these shall go away into everlasting punishment, but the righteous into life eternal.*

Beatrice thought, *What is the right thing to do? The right thing to do is to feed the hungry, give something to drink to the thirsty, give clothing to the naked, visit those who are ill, and visit those in prison.*

The Eagle continued, "What will the pagans in Persia and other countries say to the Kings of Christian countries when the pagans see the Book of Judgment that God keeps and read about the bad deeds of 'Christian' Kings?

"Holy Roman Emperor Albert the First is on the verge of committing the evil deed of invading Bohemia and devastating Prague. The pen is over God's book as it waits to record the evil deed. War kills many people, including innocent people.

"Philip the Fair will be in God's book because he brought misery to France. To finance his wars, Philip will inflate French currency and ruin many people. A sound currency is necessary to avoid misery. Philip will be thrown from his horse when a wild boar startles his horse during a royal hunt. Philip will die of the injuries incurred during the fall.

"The English and the Scots warred often, venturing into each other's territory. The Scottish leaders should stay in Scotland, and the English leaders should stay in England. Edward I and Edward II fought with William Wallace and Robert the Bruce.

"Charles II of Naples, aka Charles the Lame, aka the Cripple of Jerusalem — he was the titular King of Jerusalem and had no power there — will have his virtues and vices marked in the Book of Judgment. The Roman number I — for 1 — will be by 'Virtues' and the Roman number 'M' — for 1,000 — will be by 'Vices.'

"Frederick II of Sicily is so paltry a man that he will be allotted little space in the Book of Judgment, but the Recording Angel will need to write in shorthand in order to fit in the tiny space the records of his numerous evil deeds.

"Also recorded in the Book of Judgment among the bad Kings will be Frederick II's brother and uncle: King James of Majorca and King James II of Aragon. Both Kings disgraced their family and their kingdoms.

"Also recorded in the Book of Judgment among the bad Kings will be Orosius II of Rascia, another debaser of the coinage.

"A good king now rules in Hungary, and Hungary will be happy if it continues to escape evil.

"Navarre is happy now, and it will continue to be happy if it uses its mountains as a barrier to keep out the French."

Beatrice thought, *This will not happen. Navarre will become a part of France and will suffer under French rule just as the two principal cities of Crete suffer under Henry II, who is from a French family and who has many debaucheries that make citizens suffer. He is evil, but he is small fry. He does not run in the midst of the pack of evil beings; instead, he runs outside and beside the pack.*

Chapter 20: Jupiter — Two Pagans in Paradise (Ripheus and Trajan)

When the Sun sets, the stars become visible.

When the Eagle had been speaking, it had spoken as one. Now, it fell silent, and Dante became aware again of the individual lights who made up the Eagle.

The lights sang, and the lights grew brighter, and although the song was sweet, Dante was unable later to remember it.

The souls who were the lights loved God, and they expressed their love through their light.

A voice began to speak. The sound started in the body of the Eagle, and it sounded like the murmur of a stream. The sound then took shape in the neck of the Eagle just as music takes shape in the neck of a lute or the opening of a flute.

The sound became a voice, and the Eagle spoke through its beak: "A mortal eagle is able to look directly into the Sun. Look now at my eye. Many lights give me form, but the lights who make up my eye are the brightest and the worthiest.

"The light who makes up the pupil of the eye is David, who was a poet. He also danced before the ark of the covenant. This ark — a sacred chest — contained two tablets: On the two tablets were written the Ten Commandments. David dancing before the Ark of the Covenant is one of the exempla of humility on the first ledge of the Mountain of Purgatory.

"Now he knows the value of his poems. He contributed to them, but the Holy Spirit also contributed to them through David, whose bliss is equal to what he contributed to his poems.

"Five lights form my eyebrow. The light closest to my beak is the Emperor Trajan, who was not proud. He was just. Instead of going to war right away, he first helped a widow whose son had been killed. This story is one of the exempla of humility on the first ledge of the Mountain of Purgatory.

"Now he knows what is the penalty for failing to follow Christ. He learned that during the time that he spent in Limbo before he was permitted to enter Paradise.

"Next in the eyebrow is King Hezekiah of Judah. He learned that he was going to die of illness, but he prayed to God, 'I beseech thee, O Lord, remember now how I have walked before You in truth and with a perfect heart, and have done that which is good in Your sight.' God heard his prayer and allowed him to live for fifteen more years. God told him, 'And I will add to your days fifteen years; and I will deliver you and this city out of the hand of the King of Assyria; and I will defend this city for My own sake, and for My servant David's sake.'

"Now he knows that God's eternal laws never change — not even when God delays events because of a worthy prayer.

"The next light is the Emperor Constantine, who moved the capital of the Roman Empire east to Constantinople in 330 C.E. His doing this left the popes in charge of Rome and the Western part of the Roman Empire. This move by Constantine was disastrous because it made the popes greedy, although Constantine himself had good motives when he made his donation.

"Now he knows that the evil consequences of his action do not harm his soul because his motive was good when he acted. The evil consequences of an action — as long as one's motive is good — will not harm one's soul even if the entire world is destroyed by that action. Good motives will help people get into Paradise, and the bad consequences of actions that people do with a good motive will not keep them out of Paradise.

"The next soul in the eyebrow is King William II the Good, King of Naples and Sicily. He is a son who is better than his father: King William I the Bad. King William II was good to religious institutions and to his people, who mourned his death in 1189 C.E. The Kings who followed him — Charles II of Naples, aka Charles the Lame, aka the Cripple of Jerusalem, and Frederick II of Sicily — were bad.

"Now he knows how much Paradise loves a righteous king.

"The final light in the eyebrow is Ripheus of Troy, whom no one in your world would expect to be here. Ripheus is pre-Christian. He is mentioned very briefly in Book 2 of Virgil's *Aeneid*, which recounts the fall of Troy. Ripheus fought with Aeneas against the conquering Achaeans, and he died defending Troy. Ripheus was the most just of all the Trojans, and he was keenest for what was right. People would not expect to see Ripheus in Paradise because he lived centuries before the time of Christ, and he was not a Jew.

"Now he knows more about God's grace than any living man, although, even he, who is in Paradise, cannot see to the bottom of the depths of the mind of God."

The Eagle then sang like a lark singing in the sky, and then it fell silent, happy with the last notes of its beautiful song. The Eagle was happy to reflect God's glory.

Dante was perplexed. These souls included two Jews, two Christians, and two pagans — or at least they seemed to be pagans. How could two pagans be in Paradise?

Dante asked, "How is this possible?"

The lights flashed, happy with the opportunity to enlighten Dante.

The Eagle said to Dante, "I see that you believe that Trajan and Ripheus are in Paradise. You believe that because I told you that. But you do not see how this is possible. You do not understand the cause of their being in Paradise. To you, the truth is hidden.

"You understand the fact, but not the cause or reason. You need to have the cause or reason explained to you.

"The Kingdom of Heaven can be defeated by fervent love and by vibrant hope. In fact, God wants to be defeated in that way. By suffering defeat, God shows mercy, and by showing mercy, God achieves victory. Defeat suffered on an Earthly battlefield is very much different.

"You do not understand why Trajan and Ripheus, whom you believe to be pagans, can be here in Paradise. Actually, when they left their bodies, they were Christians. Trajan had faith in the feet that had already suffered in the Crucifixion, and Ripheus had faith in the feet that would suffer in the Crucifixion.

"The Roman Emperor Trajan lived after the time of Christ. He died in the year 117 C.E., and he did not prosecute Christians.

"Pope Gregory the Great, who died in 604 C.E., was so impressed by the story of Trajan and the woman whose son had been killed that he prayed so fervently for Trajan that the Roman Emperor was brought back to life and taken from Limbo. While alive for the second time, Trajan accepted Christ, and he then died a Christian.

"After the first time he died, the pagan Trajan went to Limbo, but after the second time he died, the Christian Trajan went to Paradise.

"Ripheus, over a thousand years before Christ, so believed in and loved justice that he received God's grace, which is so deep that no man can see its bottom.

"Because Ripheus so loved righteousness, God opened his eyes and he became a Christian. He hated the pagan gods and tried to warn the people who worshipped them that they were doing wrong."

Beatrice thought, *The pagan gods were not worthy of being worshipped. The pagan gods were powerful, but they were not omnipotent. The pagan gods knew a lot, but they were not omniscient. The pagans were far from being good. They simply did not care much for human beings. Story after story in ancient mythology recounts the gods raping mortals. If a god is to be worthy of being worshipped, that god must be omnibenevolent, and the pagan gods were not even benevolent. The one true God is omnibenevolent and is worthy of being worshipped. Ripheus realized how bad the pagan gods were and how all-good the one true God is.*

The Eagle continued, "Ripheus was baptized more than a thousand years before baptism existed. Those three ladies who were at the right wheel of the chariot — Faith, Hope, and Love — were his baptism. Ripheus believed in faith, hope, and love — the theological virtues — so much that his belief was his baptism. Of course, Ripheus' culture did not know about baptism.

"Predestination exists. From before the beginning of the existence of the universe, God knew who would be saved and who would not be saved. This does not negate free will. God sees the past, the present, and the future all at the same time, and God sees people use their free will to make decisions freely. To people, predestination is a mystery because they do not see as God sees.

"God exists outside of time and space, and so God knows our every action: past, present, and future. God sees us using our free will to either do the right thing or do the wrong thing.

"Be slow to judge, people who live on Earth. Even we saved souls in Paradise do not know who will be saved. We see into the mind of God, but we do not see so deeply that we know that.

"We are not bothered by our lack of this knowledge. We will what God wills, and we are happy with what God wills."

And so the eagle responded to Dante's questions with as much information as he was able to understand.

And the two lights who were Trajan and Ripheus quivered as the Eagle sang a song.

Dante the Poet thought, *We have limitations. We are unable to explain the mystery of predestination. We are unable to tell who will wind up in the Inferno and who will wind up in Paradise.*

None of us can make up a list of 10 things we have to do in order to get a Get-Out-of-Hell-Free card. This doesn't mean that we don't know lots of things we ought to do and lots of things we ought not to do if we want to make it to Paradise. But we would be arrogant if we were to tell God that we did such-and-such, and therefore God has to let us into Paradise.

One person who did make a list of things to do in order to get into Paradise is Guido da Montefeltro. His list included Repent and Give Up Sin, but of course he failed miserably at sincerely doing these things. Even though Guido metaphorically made his list and checked off all the items, God knew that Guido was trying to scam Him, and therefore Guido ended up in the Inferno.

Of course, Paradise does have good surprises:

A pagan from the Trojan War is in Paradise!

Someone's earnest prayer helped save a pagan who was already dead!

And since we can't figure out such things as Salvation and Predestination, perhaps other excellent surprises are in store for us.

Beatrice thought, *God is merciful and omnibenevolent: He is an all-loving God. We have a hard time understanding eternal punishment. Interestingly, some Christian mystics, including Julian of Norwich, and some Christian theologians, including Origen, believe in* apocatastasis. *They believe that all will be well for everybody in the end. In other words, everybody will make it to Paradise in the end. The word* apocatastasis *means an upset verdict — someone may have been sentenced to eternal damnation, but if that verdict is upset, then that person will make it to Paradise.*

I am in Paradise, and I cannot see deeply enough into the mind of God to know everything that will happen in the future, but if everyone, including the worst sinners of all time, eventually makes it to Paradise, it would be a triumph for Unconditional Love.

Chapter 21: Saturn — Symbolic Ladder; Saint Peter Damian

Dante looked at Beatrice. Beatrice did not smile.

She explained, "Were I to smile in this new Sphere — Saturn — you would be incinerated because you are not yet able to withstand such beauty. You would be incinerated like Semele was when the Roman god Jupiter appeared to her the way he appears to the other gods."

Dante thought, *One should not be temperate in some things. One is Love. Unconditional Love is not temperate. However, even though Beatrice's beauty is not temperate — she becomes more and more beautiful the closer she rises to Paradise — she demonstrates temperance in how she handles her beauty. For example, she does not smile at me because she knows that if she were to smile, her beauty would blast me to ashes, the way that Semele was blasted to ashes when she asked Jupiter to reveal himself to her in all his glory. In ancient mythology, mortals cannot look at gods in all their glory and survive. This may be why the gods and goddesses so often disguise themselves as mortals when they come among Humankind.*

Beatrice and I have risen to the next Sphere: Saturn, which is the planet of temperance. Temperance means moderation; it means not going to extremes. Temperance is one of the cardinal virtues. The four cardinal virtues are wisdom, courage, justice, and temperance.

Saint Thomas Aquinas regarded temperance as the disciplining of our instincts toward pleasure.

He was right.

Eating is pleasurable, but a temperate person will not be obese. Sex is pleasurable, but a temperate person will not be a rapist or engage in other kinds of immoral sex. Drinking wine is pleasurable, but a temperate person will not drink excessively.

Temperance is very important, as is shown by the fact that the planet devoted to temperance is the closest to Paradise of the planets devoted to the four cardinal virtues. Other people of my time probably regard wisdom as being more important than temperance, but I, Dante, believe differently.

Beatrice continued, "My beauty grows greater the closer I am to God. If I did not temper my beauty now, you would not be able to withstand it. Without being tempered, my beauty would hit your eyes in the same way that a lightning bolt hits a tree."

Beatrice asked Dante to look up.

Dante loved looking at Beatrice's beauty even though she was not smiling, and he loved even more obeying her. He turned his eyes away from her face and looked up.

Saturn is the name of the ancient Roman god who ruled during a Golden Age. Dante saw a Ladder. It was gold, and Saturn was silver, and the Ladder stretched so far that Dante could not see its end.

Coming down the Ladder were many lights — so many that Dante wondered whether every star in the night sky was coming down the rungs of the Ladder.

Dante thought, *Four planets are devoted to the cardinal virtues: wisdom, courage, justice, and temperance. Each planet has a symbol.*

The Sun is devoted to wisdom. Its symbol is the Circle, which is a symbol of Divine Infinity: Infinite Power, Infinite Knowledge, and Infinite Benevolence.

Mars is devoted to courage. Its symbol is the Cross, which is a symbol of Human Salvation.

Jupiter is devoted to justice. Its symbol is the Eagle, which is a symbol of Earthly Order.

Saturn is devoted to temperance. Its symbol is the Ladder, which is a symbol of Spiritual Vision.

Sometimes, crows will flock together as they warm up in the Sun after dawn. After warming up, they will move separately. Some will fly away and not return. Some will fly away and then come back to where they started. Some will fly in the same area where they warmed up.

Some contemplatives will leave their religious house and return to the world. Some contemplatives will make brief trips to the world and then return to their religious house. Some contemplatives will never leave their religious house.

The souls on the Ladder reached a certain rung, and then they stopped.

But one soul nearby glowed brightly, and Dante said to himself, "From your glowing, I can see the love you bear me, but Beatrice, who bids me when to speak and when not to speak, is quiet, and so I am not asking this soul anything, although I would like to."

Beatrice, who knew Dante's thoughts, said to him, "Satisfy your desire to ask questions."

Dante said to the bright soul, "I am not worthy to receive an answer from you, but for the sake of Beatrice, who gives me permission to ask questions, please tell me the answers to two questions. First, why did you come so close to me? Second, why are no souls singing here although souls have been singing in the Spheres below Saturn?"

The bright soul replied and answered Dante's second question first, "Because you are mortal, your hearing is limited just as your seeing is limited. The souls do not sing here for the same reason that Beatrice does not smile here. You are unable to withstand such beauty."

Then the bright soul answered Dante's second question, "I have come so far down the rungs of the Ladder simply so that I can welcome you. I am not here because I love more than other souls — you can see brighter souls on the rungs of the Ladder.

"But God's love makes us want to serve others and assigns us deeds to do. This is my assigned deed."

Dante said to the bright soul, "I understand that saved souls freely serve God and God's omnibenevolence, but how is it that you alone out of all these souls have been the one predestined to answer my questions?"

The bright soul spun around in joy at being able to speak to Dante, and the bright soul said, "God's love shines on me and joins my sight, and I can see a vision of God. From this vision of God comes my joy.

"By as much as my spiritual vision is clear, my light will be bright.

"But I cannot explain to you the answer to your question. Even the most enlightened of the Seraphim, who are the highest order of Angels and the order of Angels closest to God, cannot answer your question. The explanation you seek is hidden deep in the mind of God — so deep that no human being should seek its answer.

"A mind that is bright in Paradise is dull on Earth. How then could a human being on Earth discover an answer that a soul in Paradise cannot find?"

Dante knew that the bright soul could not answer this question, and so he humbly asked who the bright soul was.

The bright soul answered, "In Italy is the monastery of Santa Croce di Fonte Avella. In my time, it devoted itself to praising God. I served God there, and I ate nothing but plain foods prepared with inexpensive olive oil. I welcomed both heat and cold, and I contemplated God.

"This monastery produced many souls who are in Paradise, but now this monastery is decadent.

"At this monastery I was known as Peter Damian, but at Santa Maria in Porto I was known as Peter the Sinner.

"Not many years on Earth were left to me when Pope Stephen IX made me wear the hat of a cardinal — a hat that seems to pass from bad people to worse people.

"In the early days of the Church, Simon became Cephas, aka Peter. He was lean, and he was barefoot, and he ate whatever food was offered to him. Saint Peter was temperate.

"But modern popes and cardinals need help from many people to push their big butts — grown huge from too much food — up on horses. Modern popes and cardinals are so big-butted and so big in body that when they are on a horse their clothing covers the horse so that it looks like one being is under the clothing.

"God endures so much!"

When Peter Damian said these words, many souls joined him, and all the souls cried out. No one on Earth has heard such an outcry, and the outcry was so loud that Dante could not make out the words of the outcry.

Dante thought, *On Saturn, the planet of temperance, we find contemplatives such as Peter Damian. On Earth, the contemplatives contemplate God, and they may occasionally enjoy a direct experience of God.*

Peter Damian was a great contemplative who was called away from the contemplative life. He lived in the 11th century C.E., and he was a contemplative who was forced to become a cardinal although he did not want to; instead, he wanted to remain a contemplative.

Pope Stephen IX made Peter Damian a cardinal because the Pope wanted a contemplative such as Peter Damian to help him reform the Church. Contemplatives have the ability to reform. Both Peter Damian and Pope Stephen IX supported the Gregorian Reform.

Because Pope Stephen IX wanted to reform the Church, he found the best man for the job, and he made him a cardinal. (Of course, other reformers existed.) A Simonist pope such as Pope Boniface VIII would have made cardinal whoever offered him the greatest amount of money.

Compare the people who are made cardinals in the two systems. A Simonist wants to be made cardinal but is not qualified to be a cardinal. Peter Damian is qualified to be a cardinal, but he resists being made cardinal until he is convinced that he can do a lot of good as cardinal.

Why are contemplatives so often a good choice for reforming the Church?

Contemplatives are temperate. They do not overindulge in food, sex, or wine.

Why is temperance so important? Temperance is important if we are to develop and use our other virtues. Temperance is a foundation for the other cardinal virtues.

Let's say that you are addicted to food, sex, and wine. Will you be wise, brave, and just?

If you are drunk all the time, you won't read books or study or think much.

If you eat way too much, you won't be able to rescue a child from a burning house because you will be too fat to climb in the window so you can rescue the child.

If you are addicted to sex, you won't be a just judge because all a pretty (or handsome) defendant has to do to get a verdict of "innocent" is to sleep with you.

Contemplatives, being temperate, avoid these pitfalls, and they keep their eye on the prize.

Beatrice thought, *Peter Damian is a model for Dante to follow. Peter Damian was a contemplative who was able to experience God, but he left the contemplative life because the Pope needed him to help reform the Church. Similarly, Dante is going to be able to experience God. This will be his own kind of contemplative experience. However, like Peter Damian, Dante is going to have to leave. He is not ready to stay in Paradise. Instead, Dante has work to accomplish on Earth: He has to write* The Divine Comedy. *Later, after his death, is the time for Dante to stay in Paradise permanently. Like Peter Damian, Dante will be a reformer.*

Chapter 22: Saturn — Saint Benedict

Shocked by the cry of the souls, Dante turned toward Beatrice the way a little boy runs to his mother when he is startled.

Beatrice calmed Dante just like a mother would calm a son.

She said to him, "You are in Paradise, and here every act is correct. You have heard a cry of righteous zeal. Think now of what would have happened if these souls had sung or if I had smiled — all these souls did was to give a single cry of righteous zeal, and you are shaken.

"You were unable to make out the words they cried, but if you had you would know the vengeance that God will wreak against the religious who are unworthy. But I will tell you that you will witness that vengeance while you are still alive.

"God's vengeance arrives at exactly the right time, although the guilty think it arrives too early and the innocent think it arrives too late.

"But now look at the souls again. Let me speak to you and guide your eyes so that you see many remarkable souls."

Dante turned and saw hundreds of bright globes of fire; each globe was a soul. Dante restrained himself and did not speak. He wanted to speak, but he did not want to risk offending Beatrice or anyone else. He was like a Benedictine monk who would not speak until spoken to.

Then the largest, most brilliant light came forward and spoke to Dante. This light knew that Dante wanted information, and this light was willing to help Dante.

The light said to Dante, "If you knew the love we souls have for you, you would speak to us and share your thoughts. I know you have a question. Let me answer it without your asking it so that I do not cause you delay and so that you may continue your journey through Paradise.

"Monte Cassino in Italy was filled with pagans while I was alive. I was the first to be a missionary to them and teach them about Jesus Christ and the One True God.

"Grace shone on me, and I was successful as a missionary. I reclaimed for God many towns in the region. I converted the pagans to Christianity.

"The flames — the lights — around me were all contemplatives. They experienced the Divine Love that brings forth good thoughts and good deeds."

Dante thought, *This soul is Saint Benedict, and he was a sixth-century Italian monk. He is a contemplative; in fact, he is known as the founder of Western monasticism. He founded a monastery at Monte Cassino. Lots of pagans were around Monte Cassino when Saint Benedict founded his monastery there, and so Saint Benedict acted as a missionary, converting pagans to Christianity. In the Rule of Saint Benedict, which most Western Catholic monks follow, the monks are contemplatives, they live in a cloister, and they pray in a group many times a day.*

Saint Benedict continued, "These two souls here are Saint Macarius the Younger of Alexandria, who died in 404 C.E. and is known as the founder of Eastern monasticism, and Saint Romuald, who died in 1027 C.E. and helped reform Benedictinism in the 11st century. He is known as the founder of the order of Reformed Benedictines.

"And here are my brother monks who stayed in cloisters and kept a good heart."

Dante said to Saint Benedict, "Thank you for the love you have shown me by speaking to me, and thank you for all of your good intentions. You make me feel confident enough to ask you a question: Do I have enough grace to be able to see your face instead of this light?"

Saint Benedict replied, "Your desire will be fulfilled, but not in this Sphere. In the Mystic Empyrean you will be able to see my face and the faces of the other saved souls. At that time and in that space — in the Mystic Empyrean that is beyond time and space — all wishes are good and all wishes are fulfilled. Only in the Mystic Empyrean are all wishes perfect, ripe, and whole.

"Only in the Mystic Empyrean are no space and no time. The Ladder reaches to the Mystic Empyrean, and so you cannot see the end of the Ladder. Jacob is the one who dreamed about the Ladder reaching to the Mystic Empyrean and about Angels climbing it."

Dante thought, *The Ladder is a symbol of communication between God and Humankind. We read the story of Jacob's Ladder in Genesis 28:12-16. Jacob dreamed, and he saw a Ladder set up on the Earth, and the top of it reached to Paradise. He saw the Angels of God ascending and descending on it. The Ladder is also a symbol of Spiritual Vision. Each rung of the Ladder represents knowledge of the Divine that the contemplative has achieved.*

Saint Benedict continued, "But these days no one attempts to climb the Ladder. To do so would require lifting a foot from off the Earth, and this is something that people these days regard as asking too much.

"I wrote the *Regula Monachorum* [*Rule for Monks*], but since no one follows these rules, they are not worth the parchment they are written on — and neither is my Order.

"The cells that used to be for monks in my Order are now stalls for beasts.

"The cowls that monks in my Order used to wear are now rotten bags of rotten meal.

"The sin of usury is a serious sin, but even worse in God's eyes is the desire for money that makes monks insane. The monks desire money that is supposed to be used for the poor; the monks want to use the money for the monks' illegitimate children and mistresses.

"Many monks start out well but are soon corrupted. To flourish, monks must have the proper conditions. Their good beginning must last longer than it takes an oak tree to form an acorn.

"Look at how people build faith. Peter built faith without silver and gold. I built faith with praying and fasting. Saint Francis built faith with humbleness."

Dante thought, *Saint Benedict was a great missionary. Why? He was a contemplative. Contemplatives pray, and they have discipline. They have roots in spiritual discipline.*

It is a good idea for us to be also rooted in spiritual discipline. If we want to make positive changes in the world, we need to have good roots.

We can build on the work of others. People in different historical eras need different things, but we can build on the good work that has been done before us. Saint Peter did not want silver and gold. Saint Benedict stressed praying and fasting. Saint Francis was humble.

In Saint Francis' day, what was needed was humility, and so he was humble. However, he also prayed and fasted, just as Saint Benedict recommended. He also did not need silver and gold, just as Saint Peter recommended.

Did Saint Francis build a new church? No. He reformed the old church. He built on the foundations that had been made by others.

Throughout the universe are things that can lead us back to God. The founders of religious orders that I see on Saturn are people who have found things that lead us back to God.

We need to use the wisdom of other people. These contemplatives have found things that can lead us back to God, so why shouldn't we be aware of and make use of them? One of the good things that we can do in our lives is to investigate different religious orders and see what truth we can find in them.

Saint Benedict continued, "The Church needs intervention to be saved. Divine interventions have occurred before. God made the Jordan flow backwards, and he parted the Red Sea so that the Jews could escape from Egypt. These Divine interventions are much greater than the intervention that is now needed to save the Church."

Saint Benedict then withdrew, and he and the other souls swept up the Ladder like a whirlwind.

Beatrice made a gesture, and she and Dante swept up the Ladder. Her gesture made Dante's body light.

Their movement up the Ladder was fast, much faster than the speeds achieved by Humankind on Earth.

As quickly as you can remove a finger from the heat of a fire, Dante and Beatrice had risen to the next Sphere: that of the Fixed Stars. The planets move around the night sky, but the Fixed Stars are fixed into position and do not move relative to each other.

Dante and Beatrice entered the constellation of Gemini. In Dante's time, the stars and planets were thought to influence those born in their sign. Dante was born a Gemini. The people of Dante's time thought that Geminis are inclined to pursue the arts and intellectual endeavors.

Dante was happy to enter his own sign when he entered the Sphere of the Fixed Stars. He knew that soon he would pass beyond this Sphere into the Mystic Empyrean.

Beatrice said to him, "You are very close now to your destination. You will see the final blessedness, so work now to keep your vision clear.

"Look back now at the distance we have traveled. We have crossed the universe. Look back now, and soon you will know much joy."

Dante looked back, and he saw all of the Spheres that he and Beatrice had visited, and he saw the Earth, which looked so paltry that he smiled.

He thought, *In the grand scheme of things, the Earth is not worth much. The best minds will not value it highly, and the wisest men will think about things other than the Earth. The Earth is our abode for now, but it is not the center of value of the universe. The center of value of the universe is actually beyond the universe, in the realm in which God dwells.*

Dante looked at the Moon; on this side, the side not facing the Earth, it had no spots. He looked straight at and into the Sun without hurting his eyes. He saw Mercury and Venus, which were very close to the Sun. He saw Jupiter, which was temperate in between the heat of Mars and the coolness of Saturn. He was able to see how these planets moved.

He saw all seven planets that were known by medieval people. He saw that they were vast. He saw that they spun swiftly. He saw the distance between their Spheres.

He saw the Earth: a patch of dust on which Humankind commits sins.

And then he turned and looked at the eyes of Beatrice.

Chapter 23: Gemini — Christ, Mary, and the Saints

A mother bird will eagerly await dawn so that she can go forth and find food for her nestlings — this is a task that she joyfully performs.

Much like that, Beatrice looked eagerly upward, awaiting something good that she knew was soon to happen. Looking at her, Dante also became filled with eager anticipation.

Quickly, what Beatrice was awaiting arrived. She said to Dante, "Look at the Angels of Paradise who celebrate the triumphant Christ, and look at the saved souls who are the fruits of Christ's triumph."

Dante saw how bright Beatrice's face was. He saw how happy her eyes were. But the brightness and the happiness were so high in degree that he knew that he would not be able to describe them.

On a night with a full moon, nymphs surround the virgin goddess Diana. Dante saw a Sun — Jesus Christ — that outshone the other lights — the Angels and the saved souls — much like the way that our Sun that shines on the Earth outshines the stars in the night sky.

The Sun Who was Jesus Christ was so bright that Dante was not able to look at Him.

Beatrice said, "The Light Who blinds you now is so strong that nothing is or can be a defense against Him. Within that Light is wisdom and power that created a way for Humankind to go to Paradise."

Lightning springs into existence and suddenly strikes. Dante's mind swelled with the vision of Christ, and it was as if his mind were lightning, exploding and breaking boundaries. What happened to his mind Dante could not explain, except to say that it had expanded.

This kind of expansion of the mind is preparation for the experience of Divine Revelation.

Beatrice said to Dante, "Open your eyes. Look at me. What you have just witnessed has expanded your mind, and you can now look at my smile without being incinerated."

Later, back on Earth, Dante the Poet thought about this moment: *Now, trying to remember, I am like a man who has just woken from a deep sleep and has forgotten what he dreamed. But I do remember Beatrice's invitation, and that is something that I will never forget.*

But still, even if Polyhymnia, the Muse of Song, and all the other Muses were to assist me, I would not be able to describe Beatrice's smile and the glow of her holy face.

These are descriptions that I have to skip. These descriptions are ineffable.

But readers, please remember what I am trying to do in my poem Paradise. *My poem has a mighty theme, and my shoulders are mortal, and when I try to carry this theme, I stagger.*

Imagine that I am in a boat trying to cross this particular stretch of sea. This is no place for a small boat or for a boat captain who wishes to take it easy.

Beatrice said to Dante, who was still looking at her smile, "Why are you looking so intently at my face? You can see much more here. Look at the Angels and the saved souls with Jesus Christ. They are like flowers in a garden.

"And look at the Rose — the Mother Mary, in whose body the incarnation of God took place. And look at the lilies — the Apostles. The fragrance — the good words and good actions — of the Apostles led many souls to salvation."

Dante, who was eager to please Beatrice, looked at the lights.

On a sunny day, the sunshine will light a field of flowers and make colors vibrant. Dante saw many lights who were filled with love from the Light Who was brightest. This Light — Jesus Christ — had withdrawn from Dante's sight because Dante's eyes were not ready for so strong a Light.

Christ had ascended, but many other splendid lights remained. Because his mind had been transformed, Dante could now look at the many splendors who were still before him. The brightest of all these splendors was Mary, the mother of Christ, to whom Dante prayed daily. This light — a living star — Dante was able to see.

The Angel Gabriel descended, circled Mary, and sang words of praise to her.

Dante saw a ring of fire — the Angel Gabriel — spin around Mother Mary as if the Angel were a fiery crown. Gabriel sang, and the sweetest music that Humankind hears on Earth sounds like thunder compared to Gabriel's singing for Mother Mary.

Gabriel sang, "I and the other Angels love you, Mother Mary, in whose womb Jesus Christ dwelt, and I will circle you as you follow your Son to the Mystic Empyrean and make it more divine with your presence."

The other souls sang Mary's name.

Mary then left, following in the path of Jesus.

The Primum Mobile is the Sphere beyond the Sphere of the Fixed Stars. It moves the fastest of all the Spheres and is the closest to the Mystic Empyrean. Dante knew it existed and he looked for it, but it was so far away that he could not see it. Because Dante's eyes were not strong enough to see the Primum Mobile, he was unable to watch Mother Mary and the Angel Gabriel for very long as they rose higher and further away.

After an infant is finished sucking milk from his mother's breasts, the infant will raise his arms to his mother, glowing with love.

Much like that, the lights stretched their flames in appreciation of and love for Mother Mary.

And with their flames stretched, the lights sang the "*Regina Coeli*":

"Queen of Heaven, rejoice, alleluia.

"For He Whom you deserved to bear in your womb, alleluia.

"Has risen, as He promised, alleluia.

"Pray for us to God, alleluia.

"Rejoice and be glad, O Virgin Mary, alleluia.

"For the Lord has truly risen, alleluia."

These souls who are in Paradise did much good while they were alive on Earth. When they were on the Earth, they scorned gold, but now they have the grace of God.

And here, beneath the Son of God and beneath Mary and among the saved souls who lived in Old Covenant times and the saved souls who lived in New Covenant times is a victorious and triumphant soul — Saint Peter — who holds glorious keys.

Chapter 24: Gemini — Saint Peter Examines Dante's Faith

Beatrice said to the lights, "O saved souls who feast at the banquet, help this man. With God's grace give him a few crumbs that fall from the table. Consider his great thirst, and give him a few drops. Your needs are entirely satisfied."

The souls spun in circles. They were synchronized the way that wheels in clocks are synchronized. They moved in harmony, although some spun in circles quickly and others spun in circles slowly. The speed of their movement revealed to Dante the degree of their bliss.

The soul who was brightest and who spun fastest circled Beatrice three times while music played that was so beautiful that it was ineffable and Dante could not remember it later.

After finishing three circles, the soul said to Beatrice, "Holy sister of mine, I have heard your prayer to us, and I am happy to grant it."

Beatrice said to the soul, "Eternal light of the man to whom Our Lord gave the keys that open the doors to Paradise, test this man. Ask him questions about faith — the faith that enabled you to walk on water.

"You know that he has love and hope and faith, but it is fitting for him to show his knowledge of and glorify faith because the citizens of Paradise are citizens of the true faith."

Beatrice thought, *Dante will be examined on his knowledge of the virtues faith, hope, and love. The first three Spheres that Dante visited were concerned with those virtues. Moon: faith. Mercury: hope. Venus: love.*

The souls in these first three Spheres incorrectly practiced or lacked in some way the virtue associated with the Sphere they were in.

Afterward, the Sun and the Spheres beyond the Sun were beyond the shadow cast by the Earth. The souls on these Spheres (including the Sun) did not lack the virtue associated with the Sphere they were in; instead, they were outstanding examples of that virtue.

One purpose of the examination is to see what changes his journey has wrought in Dante. What has he learned by taking this journey?

Three apostles will examine Dante in the virtues of faith, hope, and love. Saint Peter: faith. Saint James: hope. Saint John: love.

Dante's examination will be similar to a medieval university exam for a bachelor's degree. The examination involves discussion, not final answers. The bachelors taking these examinations in the Middle Ages discuss whatever topic the masters examining them propose. This examination is a case of engaging oneself in a dialogue from which one can learn.

Taking an examination such as this can be a good thing. The people examining Dante are on Dante's side, and they hope that Dante does well.

Saint Peter will examine Dante in the virtue of faith. This is the same Peter who before the rooster crowed denied three times that he knew Jesus after the Romans took Jesus prisoner. Peter sinned, but he repented, and he became an effective spreader of Christianity, with the result that he knows a lot about faith and that he is now in Paradise.

Dante thought about faith while he waited for Saint Peter's first question.

Saint Peter said to him, "Good Christian, speak up. What is faith?"

Defining important words to show that you know their meaning is often a good idea. Dante glanced at Beatrice, who wanted him to do well in the exam, and then he defined faith.

Dante replied to Saint Peter, "The grace of God allows me to be questioned by you. May God's grace help me to express my answers well.

"The pen of your brother, Saint Paul, who with you set Rome on the path to Christianity, wrote in Hebrews 11:1 that faith is the substance of the things we hope for, and it is argument for those things that are not seen. In my opinion, that is the essence of faith."

Beatrice thought, *Dante has done his reading for the examination. Saint Peter is the author of 1 Peter and 2 Peter in the New Testament; these books are letters. Dante has read these books, as well as the writings of Paul, including Hebrews.*

Saint Peter replied, "You are right, but do you understand why faith is substance first and argument second?"

Dante replied, "The things that are clearly evident in Paradise are not clearly evident on Earth.

"The things we hope for are the happiness and love that come from residing eternally in Paradise. Our hope for these things rests on faith, and so faith is the substance of these hoped-for things. Faith is the foundation on which our high hopes stand.

"Once we have this faith, we can use it in argument. Faith gives us the unproven (on Earth) but true (everywhere at all times) axioms or starting points from which we can gain further knowledge."

Saint Peter was pleased by Dante's answer and said, "If all mortals on Earth understood faith so well, the faulty reasoning of flawed thinkers would be ignored."

Filled with love, he added, "You understand the definition of faith. My next question is this: Do you have faith?"

Dante replied, truthfully, "Yes, I have faith of an excellent quality. If faith were a coin, my coin would not be counterfeit."

Saint Peter then asked Dante, "The other virtues, including hope and love, rest upon faith. My next question is this: From where did you get your faith?"

Dante replied, "I got my faith from the Old Testament and from the New Testament, both of which were inspired by the Holy Spirit. Any proof compared to this proof is unconvincing."

Saint Peter then asked, "What is the evidence for the truth of what we read in the Bible? How do you know that the Bible is God's holy word?"

Dante replied, "I know that the Bible is true because of the miracles recounted in it. Nature cannot perform these miracles; miracles are in opposition to the laws of nature. Miracles are the proof of the truth of faith."

Saint Peter then asked Dante, "How do you know that the miracles recounted in the Old Testament and the New Testament actually occurred? You can't simply assume that they occurred. You need to have an argument that concludes that they occurred."

Dante replied, "I look at the Earth, and I see that much of it is Christian. If the miracles actually occurred, that is a good reason for Humankind to turn to Christianity. But if Humankind were to turn to Christianity without the existence of miracles, then that would be an even greater miracle than the miracles recounted in the Old Testament and the New Testament.

"The conclusion of my argument is that it is much more likely that the miracles recounted in the Old Testament and the New Testament occurred than it is that Humankind became Christian without the occurrence of the miracles recounted in the Old Testament and the New Testament. Therefore, I believe that the miracles recounted in the Old Testament and the New Testament really occurred.

"In other words, miracles occurred, and people became Christians. Suppose that the miracles did not occur. If people became Christians without witnessing the miracles that spurred them to become Christians, that would be even more of a miracle than the miracles we read about in the Bible!

"Thank you, Saint Peter, for spreading Christianity on Earth. Unfortunately, the vines that you planted are now thorns because many clergy are corrupt."

Dante's answer pleased the saved souls. They knew that Dante was correct about the corruptness of the present clergy, and so they sang, "*Te Deum Laudamus*" — "Let Us Praise You, God." The music they sang to is heard only in Paradise.

Saint Peter was reaching almost the last of his questions. He asked Dante, "The grace of God has helped you to answer all these questions correctly, and I am pleased by what you have said. But now tell me your creed. What do you believe? What do Christians believe? And what is the source of your belief?"

Dante replied, "Saint Peter, you entered the tomb of Jesus Christ first although younger feet than yours — the feet of Saint John — arrived at the tomb first. You are now in Paradise, and your faith has now been confirmed.

"You ask what I believe and why I believe it.

"I believe in the One True God. This God moves all the Spheres although He is Unmoved; He is the Unmoved Mover. The One True God created the universe and was not Himself created. This God has necessary existence while the universe has contingent existence. This God loves.

"I know this because of physics and metaphysics — because of the Book of Nature and philosophical and theological reasoning. I know this because truth falls from Paradise to Earth. I know this because of scripture — through Moses, aka the first five books of the Bible, and through the prophets and through the Psalms and through the Gospel and through your own letters that you wrote under the influence of the Holy Spirit.

"And I believe in the Trinity. I believe in three eternal Beings. I believe in an Essence that is both One and Three. I believe that the words *is* and *are* apply equally well to this Essence.

"Why do I believe in this Essence? The teachings of the Gospel have educated me.

"And now you know the source of my belief and why I believe the way I do.

"The source of my belief is like a spark that catches fire and shines like a star in Heaven and enlightens my mind."

Saint Peter was delighted by Dante's answer, and he sang benedictions for Dante and flew three times around him.

Dante the Pilgrim had passed this examination.

Beatrice thought, *Dante has learned much not only from holy scripture (Moses, aka the first five books of the Bible; the Prophets; the Psalms; the Gospel, and from Peter and Paul), but also from philosophers such as Aristotle. When Dante refers to God as an Unmoved Mover, he is using Aristotelian language. A combination of creed and philosophy is found in Dante's answers.*

Dante has two sources of knowledge: reason (as in logic and the study of nature, including the heavenly bodies) and revelation (as in scripture).

Humankind can learn some things through reason, and Humankind can learn other things through revelation. The two kinds of knowledge do not conflict. God created the universe, and God created the physical laws of the universe, including those that guide evolution.

Importantly, by using reason, Humankind can learn some things about God. The same is true of revelation.

Chapter 25: Gemini — Saint James Examines Dante's Hope

Dante the Poet thought, *I am writing a divine poem:* The Divine Comedy. *Both Heaven and Earth have played a part in my writing of it, and I have grown thin through the effort of writing this poem.*

I hope that the people who exiled me from Florence will read this poem and allow me back into Florence. I grew up there. I was a foe to the people who rule Florence now.

I would return as a different kind of poet. No longer am I a writer of love poetry. I am now a writer of sacred poetry about God. I am now fully mature. I would like to be crowned as a poet in my own city.

I became a Christian in Florence, and I was baptized there. I hope to return there one day.

In Paradise, Beatrice thought, *Dante hopes that his poem will allow him to return to Florence and be crowned as a poet there. Dante will never make it back to Florence. The Church of Santa Croce in Florence will have a tomb for Dante, but the tomb will be empty. Dante's body will be in a tomb in Ravenna.*

In Paradise, a light started to move toward Dante the Pilgrim and Beatrice. It came from the Sphere from which the light who is Saint Peter came.

Beatrice saw the light, and ecstatic, said, "Look! Here is Saint James! On Earth, he draws souls to Galicia!"

During the Middle Ages, many people traveled to visit Saint Peter's tomb at Santiago de Campostela, which is located in Galicia in northwestern Spain.

On Earth, a dove will settle by its mate, and the dove will coo its love for the other dove and circle around it.

Much like that, Saint James greeted Beatrice, and the two sang praises for the goodness of Paradise.

After the two souls had exchanged greetings, they stood before Dante. They were so bright that Dante could not look at them.

Smiling, Beatrice said to the light, "Illustrious soul, you are the author of the Epistle of James, in which you wrote about divine benevolence and generosity. You know about hope. You, Peter, and John were the disciples in whom Jesus placed special trust. You three are proper representatives of faith, hope, and love."

Dante thought, *Saint James spent a lot of time away from home. He is known as the great Pilgrim Saint.*

Saint James said to Dante, whose eyes were lowered because of the brilliance of the lights who were Saint James and Saint Peter, "Lift up your head and look at us. The light in Paradise will strengthen you, not harm you."

Dante lifted up his eyes.

Saint James said to him, "You have been blessed by God in being allowed to visit Paradise before you die. So that Humankind may understand what hope is, answer these questions:

"What is the definition of hope?

"To what degree do you possess hope?

"What is the source of your hope?"

Dante's guide in Paradise, Beatrice, spoke up and answered the second question for Dante — very positively. She did not want Dante to answer the question because it could seem as if he were proud.

Beatrice said, "No son of the Church Militant — living Christians — has greater hope than Dante. You can see into the mind of God, and so you know that what I say is true. Dante's hope is why he has been allowed to travel to Paradise before his living days on Earth are done.

"You asked two other questions so that Dante may educate Humankind still on Earth. He can answer these questions without self-praising himself. So let us allow Dante to speak, and may God's grace help him to answer well."

Dante was like a student who has studied hard and knows his subject. He said to Saint James, "Hope is being sure of future bliss in Paradise. The future bliss will come from the grace of God and from the good that one has done or attempted to do on Earth. Because of these things, we hope for salvation.

"I have received my hope from many sources, but I received my hope first from David, the singer of the Psalms. David sang, 'They who know Your Name will have hope in You.' All who have faith as I do know that Name.

"And in your own epistle, Saint James, you taught me to hope."

Dante the Poet thought, *Hope is important in Christianity because all of us have sinned. The Old Testament has 613 laws, and all human beings who reach the age of reason break many of those laws. And even if we believe that many of the laws do not apply to Christians today, we have broken many of the laws that remain and that we think still are applicable to our lives.*

If we focus too much on our sins, we can lose hope. We can think that we have sinned so much that we will never make it to Paradise. Faith is important to hope. If we have faith in a merciful God, then we can retain our hope.

Within the light who is Saint James repeatedly flashed a flame like strikes of lightning.

Saint James said, "Love always was inside me, and it hoped. Love was with me when I was martyred and when I left the Militant Church and joined the Triumphant Church. This love leads me to ask you this: What is the goal of hope? What do you hope for?"

Dante replied, "The goal of hope is written about in the Old Testament and the New Testament. Jesus promised something to the souls who were His friends.

"The goal of hope is eternity in Paradise. Isaiah said that saved souls will wear a double raiment in Paradise: soul and body. Paradise is a place of eternal bliss.

"Your brother, Saint John, in Revelation, writes about the white robes that denote saved souls. He makes clear the object of hope.

"I hope for my soul to be immortal and for my body to be resurrected."

The souls above Dante's head were happy with his answer, and they sang, "*Sperent in Te,*" aka "They Trust in You."

Dante the Pilgrim had passed this examination.

One of the lights above Dante's head became very bright. If the Constellation of Cancer the Crab had just one star as bright as this light, then winter — a time when the constellation is visible all night — would have a month of all days and no nights because the star would be as bright as the Sun.

Much like a young girl who rises and dances to honor a bride and not to draw attention to herself, the brilliant light rushed to join Saint James and Saint Peter.

They all danced and sang, and Beatrice watched them.

Beatrice said to Dante, "This soul lay upon the breast of the Pelican, and Jesus Christ on the Cross told him to take care of Mary after Jesus died. This soul is Saint John."

Beatrice thought, *In the Middle Ages, believers sometimes referred to Jesus Christ as the Pelican because the pelican was thought to allow its young to feed upon its blood. The pelican shed its blood for its young, and Jesus Christ shed His blood for Humankind.*

As Beatrice said these words to Dante, she continued to look at the lights who are Saint Peter, Saint James, and Saint John.

Dante had heard a tradition — which was disputed — that Saint John's body had gone to Paradise along with his soul. He stared at the light who is Saint John.

Saint John said to them, "Why blind yourself by looking for something that is not there? My body is on Earth and not yet in Paradise. My body lies with other bodies until such a time as the allotted seats in Paradise are filled and Judgment Day arrives."

Dante thought, *The rest of the souls in Paradise will be given their bodies on the Day of Judgment. Of course, this is also true of the souls in the Inferno. The souls on the Mountain of Purgatory will also receive their bodies, and they will go to Paradise.*

Saint John continued, "Only two Lights are at present allowed to have both soul and body in Paradise: Jesus and Mary. Be sure to tell this to Humankind when you return to Earth."

The dance of the lights had stopped with his words, and the song had stopped. Similarly, oars rowing in water stop at the sound of the whistle of their leader, who sounds the whistle when danger is present or when necessary to prevent exhaustion.

Dante turned to Beatrice, and he discovered that he was blind. He could not see her, although the two were close to each other and they were in Paradise!

Chapter 26: Gemini — Saint John Examines Dante's Love; Adam

Dante was blind because he had looked so intently at the bright light who is Saint John to see if he had a body. Saint John said to him, "Until you regain your sight, let us talk. Answer this question, please: On what is your soul set? And please do not worry about your sight. Your eyes are merely temporarily dazzled and are not permanently blind. Beatrice, your guide through Paradise, can restore your sight as Ananias restored Saul's sight."

Dante thought, *Love is blind, and so am I — temporarily. Beatrice will soon restore my sight as Ananias restored Saul's sight. While Saul was on the road to Damascus on his way to persecute Christians, he was struck blind, and he heard a voice say to him, "Saul, Saul, why do you persecute me?" Saul asked, "Who are you, Lord?" The voice replied, "I am Jesus Whom you are persecuting." Saul, trembling and astonished, said, "Lord, what do You want me to do?" Jesus Christ said, "Arise, and go into the city, and you shall learn what you must do." The men with whom Saul traveled took him into Damascus, where he was blind for three days and did not eat. To Ananias, a disciple at Damascus, came a vision in which Jesus Christ told him to go to Saul of Tarsus. Ananias said, "Lord, I have heard from many about this man and how much evil he has done to Your saints at Jerusalem." But Jesus Christ said, "Go to him, for he is a chosen vessel to me, to bear my name before the Gentiles, and Kings, and the children of Israel." Ananias went to Saul, put his hands on him, prayed, and cured his blindness. And Saul changed his name to Paul and started doing the work needed for him to become a saint.*

Beatrice thought, *Dante is being examined in three things: faith, hope, and love. Love — appropriately — is presented as an experience. Dante need not define love the way he defined faith and hope.*

Dante replied to Saint John, "Whenever Beatrice wishes, whether quickly or later, she can restore my sight. I saw her, and I loved her. My eyes are the gates through which I began to love her.

"You ask on what is my soul set. I love the Supreme Good. I love God. I love the Being that gives full contentment in Paradise and that is the Alpha and the Omega."

Saint John encouraged Dante to answer with more detail: "You love God. Why have you aimed your bow at this mark? What and who encouraged you to aim your bow? What and who made you set your soul on God?"

Dante replied, "I learned to love God through philosophic arguments and through revelation. Reason and revelation lead to the same conclusion. Reason is philosophical arguments, and revelation is sacred scripture. These are the things that have stamped me with the heavenly seal."

Beatrice thought, *When Saint Francis received the stigmata, he was marked with a final seal. The seal indicates many things.*

The seal indicates that Saint Francis is the genuine article. The article has not been forged. Saint Francis' Christianity has not been faked.

The seal indicates that the article is in a finished state. No more work needs to be done. Saint Francis achieved Paradise. He came as close to perfection as a human being who is not also divine can.

The seal indicates that the article has been approved. If it were not approved, the seal would not be applied to it. God approved Saint Francis' life.

Saint Francis is officially sealed. He is a fully completed work of art. On the Mountain of Purgatory, the souls of the proud were bent over like the works of art known as corbels. They were being formed into works of art. Near the end of his life, Saint Francis was a fully completed work of art.

Dante's love of God means that he is stamped with a seal much like Saint Francis of Assisi.

Dante continued, "Goodness is love, and love engenders love. The more goodness that exists, the more love that exists. The more we understand goodness, the more we are able to love. God is both the Supreme Good and the Supreme Love. Once Humankind correctly understands goodness and love, Humankind seeks and loves God.

"I have learned these things from the philosopher Aristotle, who taught me about the Unmoved Mover Who is the object of desire. I have also learned these things from Exodus 33:17, in which God said, 'I shall now show you all of My goodness.' I have also learned these things from the beginning of your own Gospel in which you write about the mysteries of Paradise."

Saint John said, "Reason proves that the highest love is God. Revelation agrees with reason. But what else draws you to love God? God is your primary love, but what are the secondary loves that draw you to love God?"

Dante knew the correct answers to the question: "I love God because God's love created the universe and myself, because Jesus Christ shed His blood on the Cross so that I might live in Paradise, and because of the hope that all the faithful and I have. All of the things, and the reason and revelation I mentioned previously rescued me from false love and directed me to True Love.

"I love each soul in Paradise. Each soul is loved in Paradise and shines with the proper measure of the brightness of this love."

Dante stopped speaking, and immediately music sounded as the souls and Beatrice all sang, "Holy! Holy! Holy!"

Dante the Pilgrim had passed the final examination.

Dante regained his sight like one who is waking from sleep. All specks in Dante's eyes were gone, and he saw better than he had ever seen before. He saw Beatrice's brightness that reached a thousand miles — and more!

He also saw a fourth light who had joined Saint Peter, Saint James, and Saint John. He asked who was the fourth light.

Beatrice replied, "The fourth light is Adam, the first man. His was the first human soul created by God."

Dante was so amazed that he bent over and nearly fell. It was if a huge gust of wind had bent him over the way it blows against the tops of trees and bends them.

Dante straightened up and said to Adam, "You are the only one who was created as an adult and was not born as a baby."

Beatrice thought, *Eve may be thought of as another human being created as an adult and not as a baby, but Dante is thinking of her as part of Adam because she was made from one of Adam's ribs.*

Dante continued speaking to Adam, "You are the father of the entire human race. I beg you to speak to me and answer those questions that you know I want to ask you."

Adam was glad to answer Dante's questions. His light trembled. He said to Dante, "You do not need to tell me your questions because I know them better than you know whatever seems most self-evident to you. I see your questions reflected in the mind of God. It reflects all things, but nothing can reflect it perfectly.

"You wish to know the answers to these questions:

"How long ago was it that I was put in the Earthly Paradise?

"How long was I without sin in the Earthly Paradise?

"Why was I banished from the Earthly Paradise?

"What language did I invent for myself to speak?

"I will answer your questions in the order of their importance.

"Why was I banished from the Earthly Paradise? The tasting of the fruit of the Tree of Knowledge of Good and Evil is not what got me banished from the Earthly Paradise. What got me banished was disobeying God's orders. Eventually, Eve and I would have been allowed to eat the fruit of this tree — is not such knowledge a good thing to have, provided that it is used to do good and to avoid doing evil? — but we pursued it too hastily. Some kinds of wisdom must be acquired at the right time.

"How long ago was it that I was put in the Earthly Paradise? I was 930 years old when I died. I spent 4,302 years in Limbo before being released by Jesus Christ during the Harrowing of Hell. I was created 5,200 years before the birth of Jesus Christ. I have been in Paradise for 1,266 years. Now, in the year 1300, I am 6,498 years old.

"What language did I invent for myself to speak? I spoke a language that became extinct before the attempt by Nimrod and his followers to build the Tower of Babel. The creations of the human mind are variable and do not last forever. The same is true of the things in nature. Humankind does communicate through speech, as it is part of human nature, but Humankind can choose which way to communicate through speech. The particular kind of language used is up to different groups of human beings. Language and words change. Until I descended into Limbo, the first circle of Hell, God was called by one name, and then God was called by another name.

"How long was I without sin in the Earthly Paradise? Not long. I came into existence at 6 a.m. By 1 p.m., God banished me from the Earthly Paradise."

NOTE by David Bruce: Adam, the first human being, says, "I was created 5,200 years before the birth of Jesus Christ." We know in the 21st century that *Homo Sapiens* probably came into existence between 200,000 and 300,000 years ago. Dante, of course, lived in the late Middle Ages.

Chapter 27: Gemini — Heaven's Wrath at the Sinful Church; The Primum Mobile

All the souls sang, "Glory to Father and Son and Holy Spirit!" This song gladdened Dante.

The entire universe seemed to smile, and it seemed as if Dante were drunk with happiness.

Dante thought, *O joy! O ecstasy! O life completely filled with love and peace! O wealth without cease and without want!*

Beatrice, who always knew what Dante was thinking, thought, *That is practically a definition of Paradise.*

The four lights in front of Dante — Saint Peter, Saint James, Saint John, and Adam — blazed, and then the light who is Saint Peter grew more intense.

Saint Peter's white light grew red. It was as if the whiteness of Jupiter had changed to the redness of Mars. It was as if a white firebird and a red firebird had exchanged feathers.

Providence then silenced all the other souls, and Saint Peter said to Dante, "Do not wonder at my change of color. The other souls will soon change color, too, as they hear my words.

"Pope Boniface VIII is called pope on Earth, but his corruptness means that the papal seat is in reality vacant. Pope Boniface VIII is a usurper of the place that is mine. He has turned Rome — the resting place of my body — into a sewer of stink and blood. Lucifer rejoices at what Pope Boniface VIII has done."

At dawn and in the evening, clouds are colored red. The souls in the Sphere of the Fixed Stars turned red. Even Beatrice turned red, just like a virtuous lady blushes with shame when hearing of the moral failings of another.

Colors also changed when Christ was crucified and the Earth darkened.

Saint Peter — his complexion colored red with anger — spoke, "I did not nourish the Bride of Christ — the Church — with blood from my martyrdom so that the Church could pursue money. The other early popes such as Linus and Cletis did not suffer so that the Church could pursue money. We endured this suffering — as did Sixtus, Pius, Calixtus, and Urban — so that we could live in Paradise.

"We early popes did not want the Church to be divided — some supporting the pope, and some supporting the Holy Roman Emperor.

"I never intended for my keys to be displayed on a pope's war banners carried by an army who war against Christians.

"I never intended for a likeness of my head to be put on a papal seal used on indulgences and on paid-for reinstatements after excommunication.

"I am both angry and ashamed when I think of these things. I and the other early popes did not engage in hurtful political practices, and we did not covet gold.

"From our place in Paradise, we look down at the Earth and we see shepherds' clothing, inside of which are greedy wolves.

"God, why do You restrain Your power and not immediately punish these evil people?

"A man from Gascony and a man from Cahors will soon drink our blood and fill your court with greedy men."

Saint Peter thought, *I am referring to Pope Clement V from Gascony and Pope John XXII from Cahors.*

Saint Peter continued, "But God will save the Church, I know, the way that He saved Rome through the hero Scipio Africanus and made it safe so that the papacy could be in Rome.

"You, Dante, when you return to Earth, make sure that you tell people what I have said."

And now the lights of the saved souls rose in the Sphere like a reversing snowfall. Dante watched them as long as he could, and eventually they had risen so high that he could no longer see them.

Beatrice said to him, "Look down, now, and see how far you have traveled."

While Dante had been in the Sphere of the Fixed Stars, time had passed and the Sphere had moved. He saw the Mediterranean. He saw Cadiz in Spain, and he saw the route that mad Ulysses had taken to the Mountain of Purgatory. He also saw Phoenicia on the Eastern coast, where Zeus, in the form of a bull, had found Europa and had then taken her to Crete on his back.

Because of the movement of the Sphere, part of the Earth was in darkness, or he could have seen more of this tiny patch of dust.

Dante, in love as ever with Beatrice, wanted to look at her. He glowed as he looked at her — nothing in nature or art could compare to her smiling face.

She smiled at him, and he rose from the constellation of Gemini, which features Castor and Pollux, the twin sons of Leda and Zeus.

They entered the Primum Mobile, but Dante could not say at what point because the Primum Mobile is uniform and undifferentiated. Dante was at the outermost of the physical universe. Beyond it — although 'beyond' and 'outside' are words that apply only to the physical universe — is the Mystic Empyrean, which lies outside time and space.

Happiness was in Beatrice's smile, and the joy of God shone on her face.

She said to Dante, "The rest of the universe derives its movement from this Sphere, which derives its movement from the mind of God, which is motivated by Love. God's mind encompasses all the Spheres, including this one. It also encompasses the Earth. Only God understands the workings of this Sphere. Humankind measures time by using the movement of heavenly bodies such as planets and stars; their movement comes from this Sphere, as I hope is clear to you.

"Saint Peter criticized greedy Popes. I will now criticize greedy people.

"Humankind is greedy today. People sink and drown in greed, and they cannot keep their head above the waters of greed.

"The will of a human being is always good at first, when the human being is very young, but the will becomes corrupt from the waters of greed just like plums become rotten when drowned by too much water.

"Little children have true faith and true innocence, but their true faith and true innocence are gone by the time a boy enters puberty and begins to grow facial hair.

"A child who still lisps will observe a religious day of fasting, but when he grows a little and can speak clearly, he stuffs his face even on religious days of fasting.

"A child who still lisps will love his mother and obey her words, but when he grows up, he prefers to see her in her grave.

"An innocent person becomes corrupt when exposed to the corruption of the Church, an institution that ought to be pure and innocent.

"Why do the sheep go astray? Because they lack good shepherds.

"My words should not surprise you — you know that you have no proper leaders on Earth. When no proper leaders exist, the people will go astray.

"But in less than 90 centuries — when January is no longer a winter month in the inaccurate Julian calendar established by Julius Caesar — a storm shall make all to rights again."

Chapter 28: Primum Mobile — The Hierarchy of Angels

Dante the Poet thought, *At this time Beatrice and I were in the Primum Mobile, the outer edge and end of the material universe. What lay ahead of us? The Mystic Empyrean!*

The Mystic Empyrean lies beyond the Primum Mobile. Actually, "lies beyond" is misleading, as the Mystic Empyrean does not exist in space and time. However, because we are human beings who exist in space and time, we have to use language metaphorically when we speak of the Mystic Empyrean.

The Mystic Empyrean is the goal of Dante the Pilgrim's journey. It is also the goal of every Christian. It is the place where God dwells. Of course, here again "place" is a word that is used metaphorically.

Here in the Primum Mobile, Dante the Pilgrim was able to look at the places he has been, and now he will be able to look ahead to where he is going.

Beatrice had finished her criticism of corrupt Humankind, to which Dante the Pilgrim had paid close attention.

Just like a person can first catch sight of a candle in a mirror and then turn to see the candle, so did Dante catch sight of something in Beatrice's lovely eyes — the eyes that had made him love her — before he turned to see that sight directly.

In the Primum Mobile, anyone who looks deeply — as do the contemplatives — will see what Dante the Pilgrim saw.

Dante saw a Point of brilliant light. The Point was like a mathematical point in that it was immaterial and nonspatial. The Point's light was so brilliant that Dante was forced to shut his eyes. Because the Point of brilliant light is immaterial and nonspatial, the smallest star that we can see on Earth looked like a Moon compared in size to the Point of brilliant light.

At times, a halo seems to surround Earth's Moon. As close as the halo is to the Moon, a ring of fire is around the brilliant Point. This ring of fire moved fast — faster than the Primum Mobile, which is the fastest of all the Spheres, moves.

A second ring of fire circled the first ring of fire. A third ring of fire circled the second ring of fire. A fourth ring of fire circled the third ring of fire. A fifth ring of fire circled the fourth ring of fire. A sixth ring of fire circled the fifth ring of fire. A seventh ring of fire circled the sixth ring of fire.

The seventh ring of fire was so large that if the rainbow of Iris, the messenger of the gods, were to be extended into a full circle, it would not be big enough to encompass the seventh circle.

An eighth ring of fire circled the seventh ring of fire. A ninth ring of fire circled the eighth ring of fire.

The further each circle of fire was from the Point, the slower it moved. The first ring of fire, which was closest to the Point, was also the brightest ring of fire. It was the closest to God: the Pure Spark of Being.

Beatrice thought, *What Dante sees now is the opposite of the "reality" that Dante thinks he sees on Earth. In that "reality," the Spheres move faster the further they are from the Earth.*

Why the difference?

Dante is now seeing Ultimate Reality, which is God-centered. Ultimate Reality is much different from the "reality" that Dante thinks he sees on Earth. That "reality" is centered on the Earth, not on God. God is at the center of Ultimate Reality. The Earth is at the center of the "reality" that Humankind sees. At the center of the Earth is Lucifer's place in the Inferno.

Beatrice helped Dante to understand what he was seeing: "You see the Point on which the heavens and nature depend.

"Look at the circle — the ring of fire — closest to the Point. It spins so fast because it is motivated by the love that comes from the Point."

Dante replied, "If the universe I see from Earth were ordered like what I see here, I would not be puzzled. But in the universe I see from Earth, the Spheres that are furthest from Earth are more Godlike and move faster. But here I see that the Sphere that is closest to the Point is most Godlike and moves fastest.

"Please explain why the two sights — the one from Earth and the one from here — are different."

Beatrice said, "The relationship between the physical world and the spiritual world is not easy to understand. If you do not understand it, it is in part because no one has seen what you are seeing here and therefore no one has tried to explain what you are seeing here.

"If you wish to be enlightened, listen carefully.

"In the material world, the course of a Sphere is wide or narrow according to how close it is to God and therefore according to how much virtue courses through it.

"A Sphere that is close to God — and the Primum Mobile is the closest Sphere to God in the material world — will have more goodness and therefore will have a greater size, and so the Primum Mobile is the largest of all the Spheres in the material world.

"The Primum Mobile in the material world corresponds to the circle that is closest to God in the spiritual world. In the spiritual world, do not look at the size of the circle; instead, look at the power of the circle. In the spiritual world, the smallest circle is the circle closest to God — the Point — and so it is the circle that has the most power.

"Nine rings of fire surround the Point. The closer a ring of fire is to the Point of brilliant light, the faster it moves. The nine whirling rings of fire are the nine orders of Angels.

"The Point of brilliant light is God, Whom you are seeing from a distance.

"This seems to you to be the reverse of what you living human beings see in nature. Living human beings in the Middle Ages see the Earth as the center, and the Spheres around the Earth become more and more divine the farther they are from Earth. Here, however, the Point of brilliant light is divine, and the rings of fire whirling around are holier the closer they are to the Point of brilliant light.

"What you are seeing now is Ultimate Reality, and not the inside-out version of reality that living human beings see on Earth.

"Of course, Ultimate Reality has God at the center — not the Earth. Circling around God are the orders of Angels."

In Italy, the wind that is thought to be the mildest sent by the god Boreas is the wind that comes from the Northeast and blows the clouds away. Beatrice's words were like a wind that blew the clouds from Dante's mind. He knew, of course, that she had spoken the truth.

And now Dante saw what seemed to be sparks in the nine rings of fire. How many sparks? A chessboard has 64 same-sized squares. Imagine that the first square is associated with the number 1, and imagine that the second square is double that: 2. Imagine that the number keeps doubling for all the remaining squares. The number arrived at that way is over 18 quintillion — a quintillion is a 1 followed by 18 zeros. The number of the Angels of the various orders in Paradise is much more than 18 quintillion — mortals cannot conceive of the actual number.

Dante heard them sing "Hosanna" to the Point Who is God, who had appointed each Angel to the Angel's position in Paradise.

Beatrice knew that Dante was confused by what he was seeing, and she explained the orders of Angels to him.

She said, "Each order of Angel is associated with a heavenly Sphere. The circle closest to the Point is the order of Angels who loves God most and has the most understanding. In the first two rings closest to the Point are the Seraphim and the Cherubim. They spin swiftly and they see God most clearly and they seek to grow closer to God. The Seraphim are associated with the Primum Mobile, and the Cherubim are associated with the Fixed Stars. The third order of Angels in the first Triad is the Thrones, who are associated with Saturn and contemplation.

"All of these nine orders of Angels have bliss equal to the depth that they are able to see the mind of God. First they see God, and then they love God. Merit determines how deeply they see into the mind of God.

"The second Triad of Angels can be visualized as flowers in bloom. Here in Paradise no frost will ever harm a flower. The second Triad of Angels sings 'Hosanna' eternally. The Dominions (aka Dominations) are associated with Jupiter and justice. The Virtues are associated with Mars and courage. The Powers are associated with the Sun and wisdom.

"The third Triad of Angels consists of the Principalities, who are associated with Venus and love; the Archangels, who are associated with Mercury and hope; and the Angels, who are associated with the Moon and faith. The orders of Angels dance, and the Angels are jubilant.

"All of the orders of Angels look toward God."

Dante the Poet thought, *When Beatrice names the orders of the Angels, she does so in threes:*

The Seraphim, Cherubim, and Thrones.

The Dominations, Virtues, and Powers.

The Principalities, Archangels, and Angels.

Three is an important number of Christianity because of the Trinity.

Of course, we can put all the Angels in three groups:

1) The good Angels in Paradise.

2) The bad Angels who rebelled with Lucifer.

3) The neutral Angels who did not take a stand and who are now in the Vestibule of Hell, rejected by both Paradise and the Inferno.

Beatrice continued, "Pope Saint Gregory the Great had a different way of listing the orders of Angels, but he was mistaken. When he reached Paradise, he realized that he had been mistaken — and he smiled! The person who listed the Angels correctly was Dionysius the Areopagite, who converted to Christianity because of the preaching of Saint Paul, who traveled to Paradise and taught Dionysius about the orders of Angels."

Beatrice thought, *Dante the Poet, as you write these lines, you are smiling, too. When you wrote* The Banquet, *you followed Gregory's incorrect arrangement of the orders of Angels, not the correct arrangement of Dionysus.*

Chapter 29: Primum Mobile — The Creation and Fall of Angels

Briefly and silently, Beatrice looked at the Point of brilliant light and the nine rings of fire circling it. Upon that Point balanced the universe. Imagine the Earth at the time of the vernal equinox when the Moon and the Sun are opposite each other: One rises, and the other sets. The universe as seen from Earth at that moment is like giant scales balanced by God.

Beatrice was able to look directly at the Point of brilliant light. At this time, Dante could not.

Beatrice said to Dante, "I will tell you what you want to know. I know what you want to ask because I see it in the place where is centered every *where* and every *when*: the mind of God.

"Why did God engage in the act of creation? He did not do it to increase His goodness. God is already infinitely good. He did it so that His creations might experience existence and share in His goodness. God created the Angels in the Mystic Empyrean; God also created all other beings and things.

"God was not idle before His act of creation because time did not exist before He created the universe: Before the creation of the universe, no 'before' or 'after' existed.

"In addition to the Angels who are pure spirit, God created pure matter and a mixture of spirit and matter. Pure matter is what makes up the Earth; it lacks spirit. The heavens are made up of a mixture of spirit and matter.

"By creating the various orders of Angels, God created reflections of Himself. When God created the Angels, He also created the heavenly Spheres and the Earth. Each order of Angels is associated with a heavenly Sphere.

"God's creation is orderly and hierarchical.

"At the top are the various orders of Angels, at the bottom is the Earth, and in between are the heavens. God's threefold creation occurred all at the same time.

"Saint Jerome was mistaken when he wrote that the Angels were created centuries before God created anything else. If you read sacred scripture carefully, you will see evidence that Saint Jerome was wrong.

"I have answered some of your questions already.

"Although God created the Angels as perfect beings, they had free will, and before you can count from one to twenty, some of the Angels, including Lucifer, rebelled against God."

Dante thought, *Interestingly, Adam took longer to sin than the fallen Angels.*

Beatrice continued, "The other Angels who were loyal to God remained in the Mystic Empyrean, and they whirl in the rings of fire.

"The reason for the Angels' rebellion was Lucifer, whom you saw at the bottom of the Inferno.

"The Angels you see here were loyal to God, and they realized that their great intelligence came from the goodness of God.

"God rewarded the loyal Angels with greater vision and greater intelligence. God gave them the light of glory so that the Angels have a direct vision of God. They received the light of glory as a gift of God, a gift that God gave them because of their merit.

"A creature who receives God's grace and lovingly accepts it is worthy of it.

"If you have understood all I have said so far, you should be able to learn much more without my help.

"But because teachers on Earth partially err when they say that Angels have understanding, memory, and will, I shall say more and correct their error.

"From the moment that the faithful Angels were created, they turned toward God and have never turned away from Him. They look into the mind of God, where all things are known, and so the Angels do not have — or need — memory, although they have understanding and will.

"Angels do not have memories because they have no need of memories. They get their knowledge directly from God, so they have no need to memorize things.

"Humans often say that the Angels have memory. Some humans say this and believe it; some humans say this and do not believe it. All who say this are mistaken, but those who say it and do not believe it are more greatly at fault.

"Humans try to philosophize and sometimes they get things wrong; by trying to show off, they get off the true path.

"Philosophy can be used correctly, and it can be misused. It is misused when it is used simply to score points against someone else. It is used correctly when it is used to find out the truth.

"Arguments can be made sincerely, but bad arguments can be used deviously to mislead others.

"Philosophy is very useful. It can be used to understand whatever can be understood by human reason.

"Being an intellectual can be dangerous unless you use your intelligence and knowledge to seek the truth that can be understood by human reason. If you use your intelligence and knowledge to score points against others or to put on a show of how smart you are, then you are misusing your intelligence and knowledge.

"Even worse than engaging in bad philosophy is to ignore or misinterpret sacred scripture.

"Bad philosophy and bad theology lead to bad preaching. Bad thinkers and preachers teach incorrect things about God.

"Today, living human beings do not care about the blood that was shed to spread sacred scripture. They don't care about the happiness that comes from correctly interpreting sacred scripture.

"They try to impress other people by making up falsehoods that they call 'truths' — they ignore the Gospel and do not mention it.

"For example, some of these bad preachers say that the Moon wandered from its natural course and caused an eclipse when Jesus Christ died on the Cross.

"These bad preachers lie! The truth is that the light hid itself, and so darkness was everywhere on Earth and not just on the part of the Earth that would have been affected by an eclipse. The darkness affected Spain and India as well as Jerusalem.

"Bad preachers shout such fables from the pulpit. More such fables are shouted in one year than the number of people named Smith and Jones in a city.

"The sheep want to be fed real food, but bad preachers feed them air. The sheep know no better, and the preachers' ignorance is no excuse.

"Christ did not tell his disciples, 'Go and preach ignorant garbage to the world.' Christ wanted His disciples to teach the truth and build on it.

"Christ's disciples went forth and preached the Gospel, but today bad preachers try to be comedians and get laughs. As long as their audience laughs, bad preachers are satisfied with and proud of their bad preaching.

"But the people they are preaching to should not be satisfied. If they knew what the truth was, they would know that a bad preacher is selling goods that are like the false indulgences that bad monks carry in the long hanging tip of their hoods and sell to the ignorant. The black bird that hangs around such bad monks is Lucifer."

Beatrice thought, *Dante will know what I mean. In his medieval world, Lucifer is often depicted as a black bird that has the wings of a fallen Angel.*

Beatrice continued, "Human beings tend to be gullible, and others sometimes innocently and sometimes not so innocently take advantage of them. Saint Anthony's emblem is a pig, and people used to allow the pigs of monks to fatten on public land. Sometimes, monks gave these people pardons to show gratitude, but pardons must be given for a better reason. Sometimes, monks sold false pardons so that they could give the money to their concubines and illegitimate children.

"But enough. This is a digression from the topic of Angels. Let us return to that topic.

"Mortals cannot count the number of the unfallen Angels. Mortals cannot conceive such a number. What does Daniel 7:10 in the King James Version say about the numbers of the unfallen Angels? This: '*A fiery stream issued and came forth from before him: thousand thousands ministered to him, and ten thousand times ten thousand stood before him: the judgment was set, and the books were opened.*' A specific number is not intended in these 'thousand thousands' and 'ten thousand times ten thousand.'

"Each Angel is different. God shines His light on each of them. Each Angel receives God's light in the Angel's own way. Each Angel has a capacity for loving God, and each Angel's capacity is different from that of the other Angels.

"Each Angel is a mirror that reflects God's light."

Chapter 30: Mystic Empyrean — The River of Light; The Mystical Rose

When the Sun is over India, dawn arrives in Italy. As the Sun rises, the stars disappear. The faintest stars disappear first, and the brightest stars disappear last. Much like that, the ring of fire furthest from the Point of brilliant light disappeared, and finally the ring of fire closest to the Point of brilliant light disappeared.

When the nine rings of fire had disappeared, Dante looked at Beatrice with love.

He had often seen and described her beauty, but if he were to gather up all his praises into a poem, the poem would not come close to giving her present beauty the praise it deserved.

Beatrice was at her most beautiful; she and Dante were now in the Mystic Empyrean: the dwelling place of God, Who outshines all other lights. Her beauty was ineffable; the only One Who could properly describe it would be the One Who made it.

Dante the Poet thought, *I am defeated. I cannot describe Beatrice's beauty. No poet — whether writing in a common style or in a lofty style — has ever been so defeated as I am at this moment.*

Sunlight can make weak eyes blind, and my memory of Beatrice's beauty and her smile defeats my attempt to describe them.

I have been able to describe in poetry Beatrice's beauty from the first time I ever saw her on Earth throughout much of our journey through the heavenly bodies, but now I am forced to give up trying to describe her beauty in my poetry. If any poet can do it, that poet will have to have a far greater talent than mine.

I now need to use my poetic talent to bring the great theme of The Divine Comedy *to an end.*

Beatrice, Dante's guide, said to him, "We have reached the end of our journey. Before, we were in the greatest Sphere: the Primum Mobile. Now, we are in the Heaven of Pure Light: the Mystic Empyrean. Here, we have the light of intellect, which is never-ending Love. Here, we have Love of the True Good and the True God, and we feel bliss — a bliss that transcends all other blisses.

"Here, you will see the two hosts who dwell in Paradise: the Angels and the saved human beings. And you will see the saved human beings not as points of lights, but in their human shape, as they shall appear on Judgment Day when you will see them again."

Dante thought, *I am saved. I will return to Paradise. Beatrice has told me the wondrous things that I will see when I die and return to Paradise.*

Lightning can strike and stun our eyes. Much like that, living light enveloped Dante, and he saw nothing but light.

Beatrice said to him, "God in His Love is preparing you so that you may see properly in the Mystic Empyrean."

Dante heard Beatrice's words, and suddenly he was aware that all his senses, including sight, were supernaturally improved. Now he could see — really see. No light, no matter how bright, could blind him.

Dante saw a flowing river of light in between two banks on which were flowers bathed in the colors of Spring. From the flowing river of light, sparks of light flew upward and outward to the flowers that resembled rings of gold set with rubies.

After reaching the flowers, the jewels of light — seemingly drunk with fragrance — returned to the river of light. As one jewel entered the river, another jewel flew upward and outward.

Beatrice said to Dante, "I see in you the urgent desire to understand what it is that you are seeing. The more urgent your desire to understand, the more pleasing it is to me.

"In order to understand what you are seeing, you need to drink from the river of light — drink from it with your eyes. Only then can your thirst for understanding be satisfied.

"You see a stream of light, and you see moving jewels and a host of flowers. They approximate reality, but true reality is within your grasp. Your sight is still defective, but it can be amended by drinking from the stream."

Dante bent down to drink with his eyes from the stream of light as eagerly as an infant who has slept a long time seeks his mother's milk.

As soon as Dante's eyes had drunk from the stream of light, it changed. It used to be a straight river, but now it was round. People at a masquerade are hidden until they take off their masks. Much like that, the river revealed its true reality, as did the sparks and the flowers.

Dante saw the two hosts of Paradise. He saw that the flowers were the saved souls of human beings, and he saw that the sparks were Angels.

God had given Dante the gift of seeing the Mystic Empyrean, and now Dante prayed to God to help him describe what he was seeing.

In Paradise the light of God shines, and by the grace of God, the Angels and the saved humans are able to see that light.

The light of God reaches and is reflected from the Primum Mobile. That light of God moves the Primum Mobile, which then imparts motion to all the other Spheres.

The reflection of light is circular and vast.

On Earth, a lake can reflect a hillside with flowers and grass. Much like that, within the light of God are reflected saved souls, who sit in tier after tier — more than a thousand of them reaching upward — in the Mystic Empyrean.

The laws of nature do not apply in the Mystic Empyrean, which is not material. Dante's eyes were able to clearly see vast distances. He saw every soul in every tier, and he knew the degree of bliss that they were enjoying according to their merit. Distance did not matter. In the Mystic Empyrean, God does not use agents such as the laws of nature: God rules directly.

The tiers upon tiers were a Celestial White Rose of saved souls.

Beatrice took Dante into the golden center of the White Rose — into the circle of light, around which the petals, aka saved souls, of the Rose praise God.

Beatrice said to Dante, "Look at the saved souls in their white robes. Look at how vast is our City. Look at the seats that are filled in the tiers, and see how few seats are left empty.

"Look at this empty seat: It has a crown above it. You are able to look at it even before you die and enter Paradise for good. That seat is reserved for Henry, a great man. He will go to Italy to set things right, but the time for setting things right will not yet have arrived.

"Italy will be like a stupid child who is hungry but pushes the wet nurse away. Henry will want to do great things for Italy, but he will not be allowed to do them.

"In public, the pope of that time will pretend to be on Henry's side. But in private, he will undermine Henry.

"God will not permit the pope of that time to remain in the Holy Office. The pope will quickly end up in the Inferno among the Simoniacs, and he will push Pope Boniface VIII deeper underground!"

Dante the Poet thought, *These were Beatrice's last words to me in Paradise. Her words were bitter.*

Beatrice thought, *Henry is Holy Roman Emperor Henry VII. Of course, now, in 1300, he is still alive; therefore, he is not in the Rose right now. When Henry VII becomes Holy Roman Emperor, he will go to Italy, something that Pope Clement V will not like. A power struggle will go on over who will control Italy.*

In a perfect Italy, the Holy Roman Emperor would control secular matters in Italy, while the pope would control religious matters in Italy.

Unfortunately, Henry VII will die in 1313. Henry VII would have done good things for Italy had he lived.

Pope Clement V, who opposed Holy Roman Emperor Henry VII, will end up in the Inferno, in the circle devoted to punishing the Simoniacs.

Chapter 31: Mystic Empyrean — Saint Bernard

Dante looked and saw the White Rose, and making up the White Rose was the host of the saved souls: those whom Christ had made His own with the Cross. Some of these souls had made appearances to Dante in the physical Spheres, although they had been and were really in the Mystic Empyrean.

And he saw the other host: the Angels who soar between God and the saved souls. The Angels celebrate God Who made them, Who loves them, and Whom they love. The Angels were like bees who go to flowers and then return to the hive of Paradise. They visit the host of saved souls and then return to God: the source of love.

The faces of the Angels were red, their wings were gold, and their bodies were whiter than the snow that falls on Earth.

The Angels go back and forth from the souls and from God. They bring graces from God to the souls, and they bring praises from the souls to God.

The Angels did not block the light of God from Dante's eyes. On Earth, if a body comes in between a person and the Sun, the light of the Sun is blocked. Such laws of nature are not found in the Mystic Empyrean.

God's glory is seen in the entire universe. In some places His glory can be seen more clearly. In some places His glory can be seen less clearly. Merit determines whether God's glory is seen more clearly or less clearly in human beings. This applies to the physical universe, and it applies to the Mystic Empyrean, but in the Mystic Empyrean, God's glory is very clearly seen in all souls, although it is more clearly seen in some souls than in others.

In this kingdom of joy, the saved souls, whether from Old Testament times or from newer times, all looked upon the same goal: God. This Sole Light was also a Triune Light. This Light is the source of joy, and this Light is needed now on Earth.

Imagine barbarians coming to Rome for the first time and looking at its splendors and monuments and art. Such barbarians would be amazed. Imagine how much more amazement struck Dante — who had come to Paradise from Earth. Imagine how much more amazement struck Dante — who had come to

Paradise, a place filled with sane people, and had left Florence, a place not filled with sane people.

Dante was stupefied by what he was seeing, and he was joyful because he was seeing it. He was happy that no one — not even Beatrice — was speaking to him until he had a few moments to stare.

Dante was like a pilgrim who had reached the end of his journey and was standing in the temple, and he was trying to fill his memory so that he could describe what he had seen to the people back home.

Therefore, Dante tried to look everywhere. His eyes sought to see all the saved souls; his eyes went from tier to tier, up and down, and from side to side and back again. He saw faces that were filled with love and clad in white robes and light and smiles.

Dante had seen the major parts of Paradise, but not its details, and wanting to ask questions, he turned to his side, expecting to see Beatrice, but she was not there!

Instead, he saw an elder who wore the white robes of the saints of Paradise. He had the love of a father, and he had the joy of a saved soul.

Dante asked him, "She — where is she?"

The elder replied, "Beatrice asked me to leave my seat in the Rose and help you complete your journey by making sure that you see everything that you need to see. You can see Beatrice in the Rose; she is in the third from the highest tier. That is the place that her own merit deserves."

Dante did not speak; instead, he raised his eyes and looked at Beatrice in all her glory. Beatrice was far away, but Dante clearly saw her. Such clarity of vision at such a distance is not possible on Earth.

Dante thanked her in his thoughts, knowing that Beatrice would learn his thoughts by looking into the mind of God: "Lady, thank you for going into the Inferno to talk to Virgil and leaving your footprints there so that I might be saved. Because of your good deed, I have seen Paradise, and I recognize the excellence of all things here.

"You have led me from bondage to freedom, from exile to home. To do so, you have done everything that you are able to do. I hope that I can be as generous as you have been so that when I return to Paradise, my soul may please you."

Beatrice looked at Dante and smiled, and then she looked at God.

The elder said to Dante, "The final stage of your journey is at hand; your final lessons must be learned. To bring this about, sacred love and prayer have sent me. You still have not seen everything that you need to see. You still are not seeing God directly; you are seeing a reflection of God.

"You will receive help from Mary, the mother of Jesus and the Queen of Paradise. I know that this is true. I am devoted to Mary. I am Bernard."

Dante the Pilgrim thought, *My new guide is Saint Bernard of Clairvaux. He lived in the 12th century, and he was a member of the Cistercian religious order. Saint Bernard was a contemplative. He was a reformer. As a reformer, he wrote the pope. He advised the pope to focus on spiritual things and to cease his focus on political things. He was a preacher, and he was a poet.*

Bernard called for the Second Crusade. In that crusade, Cacciaguida, my ancestor, died a martyr.

Twenty-one years after his death, Bernard was canonized.

Dante the Poet thought, *Saint Bernard is the final guide of Dante the Pilgrim — a younger me. Each of the guides helps prepare me — that is, the Pilgrim — either for the next guide or for my final vision. Virgil got me ready to be guided by Beatrice. Beatrice got me ready to be guided by Saint Bernard. Saint Bernard will get Dante the Pilgrim ready to see God.*

Each of my three major guides — Virgil, Beatrice, and Saint Bernard — has important knowledge. Virgil knows Human Reason. Beatrice knows Revelation. Saint Bernard knows Mystical Contemplation. Saint Bernard will prepare Dante the Pilgrim to see God more clearly. Only Mystical Contemplation can do that. Saint Bernard himself had a vision of God during his lifetime.

A fervent Christian from a faraway place like Croatia may go as a pilgrim to see the Veil of Veronica: a piece of cloth on which Christ wiped the blood and sweat away from His face as He walked to be crucified on Calvary. That cloth bears the true image of Christ, and the pilgrim from Croatia looks at it, amazed at seeing how Jesus looked.

Dante felt much like that as he looked at Saint Bernard, who — while still living — had seen a vision of God as he contemplated.

Saint Bernard said, "You are a son of grace; you have received an important gift from God. However, you have more to see, and you will not see it as long as you are looking at me.

"Raise your eyes high. Look up at the highest tier. Look up at Mary, the Mother of Christ and the Queen of Paradise."

Dante raised his eyes. At dawn, the East is much brighter than the West. Dante looked at Mary, and just like the East outshining the West, she outshone the other souls.

The Sun at noon outshines everything around it. Just like that, Mary outshone all the souls on either side of her.

And around the brightness that is Mary, Dante saw more than a thousand Angels with outstretched wings — each Angel had a unique personality and a unique art and a unique motion.

And Dante saw Mary, smiling at the Angels, beautiful with a beauty that was reflected in Saint Bernard's eyes.

Dante the Poet thought, *I remember Mary and I remember Mary's beauty, but even if I had the words to describe the least part of her beauty, I would not.*

Saint Bernard saw Dante the Pilgrim looking devotedly at Mary, and he turned to Mary and looked at her with so much love that Dante had even more devotion in his gaze.

Chapter 32: Mystic Empyrean — Saint Bernard and the Saints in the Rose

Still contemplating Mary, Saint Bernard — Dante's newest guide — wanted Dante to study the Mystic Empyrean with all of its saved souls and good Angels.

Saint Bernard said to Dante, "Eve caused a wound when she ate the fruit of the Tree of Knowledge of Good and Evil. She deepened the wound when she tempted Adam to also eat of the fruit. Mary closed that wound by giving birth to Christ, who suffered on the Cross to redeem Humankind and to heal original sin.

"Eve, who is beautiful and was directly created by God, sits at the feet of Mary.

"Sitting underneath Eve in one of the thrones of the third tier is Rachel, and Beatrice is by her side. Rachel is known for her contemplation, and Beatrice brought revelation to you.

"As you look down the tiers, you see more Hebrew women. Sarah is the wife of Abraham and the mother of Isaac. Rebecca is the heroine who killed Holofernes, the general of King Nebuchadnezzar. Ruth is the great-grandmother of David, the writer of the Psalms, who wrote '*Miserere mei*' — 'Have mercy on me.'

"This half of the Rose is complete. It is the half that is made up of pagans such as Ripheus and Old Testament souls such as Adam. Many, many Jews are in Paradise."

Dante thought, *These words appear in Psalm 51:1: "Have mercy upon me, O God, according to Your lovingkindness: according to the multitude of Your tender mercies blot out my transgressions."*

In the Dark Wood when I first saw Virgil, I said, "Miserere mei." The souls in Prepurgatory also sing the "Miserere" as a way to prepare themselves to purge their sins. It is one of the ways that they get ready for Purgatory.

Of course, the souls in the Rose are the souls of the Blest. They are the saved souls who reside in Paradise forever.

Saint Bernard continued, "You can see all these souls as I go downward from tier to tier. Down from where I started is a line of Hebrew women. This vertical line and the vertical line directly opposite them divide the White Rose into two equal parts.

"On the side of the line in which I mentioned the names of a few souls are the souls who believed in the Christ Yet to Come. They lived in pre-Christian times. All of the seats are filled in this part of the White Rose.

"On the other side of this line are those who believed in Christ Already Come. They lived in Christian times. Here are some empty seats. Not all of the seats are filled in this part of the White Rose.

"On the opposite side of this line, John the Baptist sits facing Mary, Mother of God. John was always holy. He suffered in the desert, and he was martyred, and spent two years in Limbo before Christ rescued him during the Harrowing of Hell.

"Sitting in the line below John the Baptist are other saved souls. Saint Francis sits below John the Baptist. Saint Benedict sits below Saint Francis. Saint Augustine, who became the Bishop of Hippo in 396 C.E. and who is the author of *City of God* and *Confessions*, sits below Saint Benedict.

"Saint Francis is the perfect imitation of Christ, Saint Benedict is a contemplative, and Saint Augustine is a theologian.

"Others are also sitting down the line.

"The half of the White Rose that is not yet complete is devoted to those who believed in Christ Who had Come. These souls are from the New Testament onward.

"Marvel at how God has organized the White Rose. The seats for saved souls who believed in Christ Yet to Come are equal in number to the seats for saved souls who believed in Christ Who had Come."

Dante thought, *Contrasts are in the Rose: young and old, male and female, Old Testament figures and New Testament figures. The wisdom I saw on the Sun involved complementarity. We have complementarity here in the Mystic Rose.*

Saint Bernard continued, "Down from the horizontal center row are saved souls who were saved not through any merit of their own. These are children. They died before they reached the age of reason. They are saved through the mercy of Another and through the merit of others.

"Some of these children died after they were baptized, and some of these children died before baptism existed. Sincere prayers for the dead are heard in Paradise. God knows what He is doing.

"Look at the faces of these children, and listen to their voices. You will know that what I say is true.

"You have some doubts, some questions. Let me try to explain things better.

"Here in the vastness of Paradise, no mistakes are made and nothing by chance occurs. Chance is not present here just as sorrow is not present here, thirst is not present here, and hunger is not present here.

"From before the beginning of time, God has known who will dwell here.

"The souls of children are arranged in tiers that seem to indicate merit, but since these children never reached the age of reason, they have no merit. Nevertheless, everything here is like a perfect fit between a ring and a finger.

"God knows how much bliss these children are able to enjoy, and they receive exactly as much bliss as they can enjoy. Every child in Paradise is happy, and every adult in Paradise is happy.

"God determines each soul's place in Paradise. This is all we need to know.

"Holy scripture itself shows that children — even twins — are different. Jacob and Esau were twins, but they fought even in their mother's womb.

"God gave each one the grace he deserved. To you, it may seem as if he judged them according to the color of the child's hair, or for some trivial reason, but again I say that God knows what He is doing.

"The children are seated not according to their good deeds because they were too young to have done good deeds; instead, they are seated according to God's knowledge from before the beginning of time and according to God's grace.

"During the beginning centuries of the existence of Humankind, all that was needed to save the souls of the children was the faith of their parents.

"After this age was completed, for male children to be saved, circumcision was needed.

"After this age was completed, and Christ had been incarnated and crucified, baptism was needed for entry to Paradise, or the child would be sentenced to Limbo.

"Look now at Mary, who most resembles Christ. Only with Mary's help can you look at Christ."

Angels — intelligent beings of pure spirit — attended Mary. This sight spellbound Dante. Of all the faces that he had seen in Paradise, Mary's face seemed most Godlike.

With his wings spread wide, an Angel now sang to her, "Hail, Mary, full of grace." The other Angels and the saved souls joined their voices to his for the remainder of the song.

Dante asked Saint Bernard, "Holy father, you who left his seat in the White Rose to help enlighten me, please answer this question: Who is that Angel who looks into Mary's eyes with joy, who is so filled with love that he seems to burn like a fire?"

Saint Bernard, who loved and loves Mary, said, "This Angel possesses as much love and joy as is possible for any soul or Angel to possess, and all Angels and all saved souls agree that this is fitting because this is the Angel Gabriel, who appeared before Mary on Earth to announce that she would give birth to the Messiah.

"Now let me explain more about the souls in the White Rose. I will point out to you some of the great patricians.

"Sitting at Mary's left side is Adam, the Father of Humankind and the man who sinned by eating without God's permission the fruit of the Tree of Knowledge of Good and Evil. Sitting at Mary's right side is Saint Peter, the Father of the Church and the man to whom Christ gave the keys of Paradise.

"They are the two roots of the White Rose.

"Saint John the Evangelist in his Revelation prophesied hard times to come for the Church. He sits by Saint Peter's side.

"Moses sits before Adam. Moses led those who ate manna; they were difficult to lead.

"Across from Saint Peter sits Anna, who does not look at God, but instead looks with love at Mary, her daughter. She is happy as she looks at Mary and sings Hosanna.

"Facing Adam is Saint Lucia, who helped to save your soul when you seemed determined to go to Hell after your death. Saint Lucia went to Beatrice, at the request of Mary, and asked her to talk to Virgil in Limbo as a last-ditch effort — that succeeded — to save your soul.

"But now your time in Paradise is coming to an end. Let us be like a good tailor who uses the cloth he has to the best advantage.

"Let us turn our eyes upon God: the Primal Love.

"You need to look at God directly. You need to penetrate as deeply as you can into His Radiance.

"But lest you backslide into pride by thinking that you can achieve such a vision through your own merit, let us offer a prayer that asks for the gift of directly seeing God. One here has the power to help you directly see God.

"Say the prayer with me. Repeat my words in your heart sincerely."

Saint Bernard began to pray.

Chapter 33: Mystic Empyrean — Saint Bernard Prays to Mary; The Trinity and Christ's Dual Nature

Saint Bernard began his prayer with the language of paradox — actually, a trinity of paradoxes: "You, Mary, are the Virgin Mother. You, Mary, are the daughter of your son. You, Mary, are the most humble and the most exalted of all creatures."

Beatrice thought, *A paradox occurs when two ideas that normally do not belong together are put together in such a way that they result in a true insight. The language of paradox is not the language that we use in everyday life. A new kind of language is needed to describe the things that are in Paradise. They are ineffable — they cannot be described adequately in words. To try to describe them, people must use language that is not ordinary language.*

Saint Bernard continued, "You, Mary, ennobled human nature with your merit to such an extent that God consented to become incarnate in your womb. God had partially withdrawn from Humankind after the original sin of Adam and Eve, but in your womb God's love for Humankind was rekindled. God's love made the White Rose possible.

"Here in Paradise you inspire love in all of the saved souls, and on Earth, you inspire hope. In Paradise, all is love.

"Mary, you are great and powerful. People who pray look to you to give their prayers wings so that they rise upward to God.

"When people ask you for help, you give it, and often you give help without being asked.

"You are tender, you feel pity, and you are generous. You have all of the good qualities that God's created beings can have.

"This man here — Dante — has traveled from the deepest part of the deepest circle of Hell, from the bottom to the top of the Mountain of Purgatory, and from Sphere to Sphere of the Heavens, all the while talking to and learning from souls, and now he begs you to grant him one final gift: to intercede with God so that his vision may be strengthened so that he can directly see God.

"I pray for this, also. I fervently burned to have my own vision of God, and now I fervently burn to have Dante see God. I pray to you to grant my desire: to let Dante not be blind because of his own mortality, but instead to let Dante open his eyes and see God.

"I also pray to you, Mary, to protect his mortal senses and not let him be harmed when he sees God.

"And I pray to you to protect Dante from harm once he has returned to Earth. Protect him from such things as pride. The temptation to be proud can be strong for one who receives such a gift as the one I am asking you to grant him.

"And not just I am doing the asking. All of the saved souls in Paradise, including Beatrice, are now praying to you, Mary. Their hands are clasped in prayer, and they are praying that my prayer be granted."

Mary looked at Saint Bernard, and her look showed that his prayer pleased her, and then she looked at God. No one can look as deeply into the mind of God as Mary.

Dante burned to see God face to face. He raised his eyes.

Saint Bernard smiled and gestured for him to look up at God, but Dante was already looking. Dante's vision was growing clearer, and he was beginning to see into the mind of God.

Dante the Poet, back on Earth and writing *The Divine Comedy*, thought, *What I saw reached such heights that both memory and language fail me.*

I am like a person who has had a dream and has woken up. Although he cannot remember the dream, he still feels the effect that the dream had on him.

The vision I had fades, but I can still remember the sweetness I felt while having the vision.

Other things fade in the same way. Footprints made in the snow fade when sunshine strikes the snow. The Sibyl would write down her prophecies on leaves, and their meaning would fade when the wind blew and mixed up the leaves.

Now, God, I pray to You as I write: Please give me back a small part of what I experienced when I saw You face to face in Paradise. Let me remember now a small part of what I saw then. And I pray to You to give me enough command of words to reveal to future generations even one small spark of Your Being.

God, if knowledge of Your Being can return briefly to my mind, and if my words can capture even a small part of Your Being, men will know more about Your might.

I remember looking at the Eternal Light. The Light strengthened me so that I was able to see it. If I had looked away from the Light, my senses would have been overpowered and I would have fainted.

I remember that I kept looking at the Eternal Light. My strength grew, and my vision grew.

I remember that my vision united with the Eternal Light. By the grace of God, I saw within the mind of God.

I remember that contained within the mind of God is a book bound by love; that book is the universe. And in the mind of God are all forms and all essences of things. The essence of all things is found in the mind of God. I saw also substance, aka matter, and accident, aka the phases of matter, conjoined and how the two are related. And my words now can give only a hint of what I knew then.

I remember that I saw the conjoining of the temporal and the eternal in the mind of God. I know that I saw that because now as I write this, my heart is joyful.

But in one instant I forgot more than has been forgotten in the 2,500 years since Neptune, god of the sea, looked up in the water and saw the keel of the Argo, the first ship, which took Jason and his Argonauts on their journey to find the Golden Fleece. Both Neptune and I saw something marvelous, but the journey of the Argo 2,500 years ago can be remembered with more clearness than I can remember what I saw recently when I looked into the mind of God.

But my mind looked deeply and intently, and the more it saw, the more it wanted to see.

Anyone who looks within the mind of God is transformed and never wants to look away. In the mind of God is everything that is good. If something is not within the mind of God, then that thing is defective.

But now, when I describe the little that I remember of my vision, my words are like the babbling of a baby that still feeds at the mother's breasts. My words are mere baby talk.

God is perfect, and God never changes, but as my ability to see deeper into the mind of God grew, my experience of God's perfection changed. Paradise is never boring. In Paradise, we experience more and more of God's infinite perfection. That perfection never comes to an end, and no matter how much God reveals to us of His perfection, more of His perfection remains to be revealed.

I remember that I saw three circles of different colors all occupying the same space. The first circle reflected the second circle, and the first and second circles reflected the third circle. The Father begets the Son, and the Father and the Son produce the Holy Spirit.

My words as I try to describe this are weak, and "weak" is too weak a word to describe my words' weakness!

Only God fully understands the mind of God, and God fully loves.

I remember that I looked at the three circles, and one of the circles bore the image of a Man — the incarnation. I stared.

A geometer can try to square the circle — something that is impossible. I remember that like that geometer I tried to understand this new mystery, to understand how the image of a Man can fit in the circle. But my finite human mind could not understand.

I remember that a flash of understanding hit me, and I saw and I understood. I cannot tell you what I saw and understood, but I experienced and felt the Infinite Love that moves the Sun and the other stars.

Appendix A: Background Information

• Who was Dante Alighieri?

Dante, of course, is the author of *The Divine Comedy*. He was born a Roman Catholic in Florence in 1265 C.E. He died of malaria in Ravenna, Italy, in 1321 (the night of Sept. 13-14). He remains buried in Ravenna, although an empty tomb in Florence is dedicated to him. Dante is known for his ability as a world-class poet, for his interest in politics, and for being exiled from Florence. In a way, he remains exiled from Florence, as his body is not in a tomb in Florence.

• What is *The Divine Comedy* in essence?

The Divine Comedy tells about Dante's imaginative journey through the afterlife. Dante finds himself in a dark wood of error, and his guide, Virgil, the author of the Roman epic the *Aeneid*, takes Dante through the Inferno (Hell), and up the Mountain of Purgatory to the Forest of Eden. There Beatrice, Dante's beloved who died early in life, takes over as Dante's guide, and the two ascend the spheres of Paradise, until finally Dante, with the aid of another guide and of the Virgin Mary, is able to see God face to face. These three parts of Dante's imaginative journey make up the three parts of *The Divine Comedy*: the *Inferno*, the *Purgatory*, and the *Paradise*.

In *The Divine Comedy*, Dante tells the reader how to achieve Paradise. In addition, the epic is a love story. A woman saves Dante.

• How long does the journey in *The Divine Comedy* take?

Considering all the distance that is traveled, it doesn't take long at all. It begins on the night before Good Friday and ends on Easter Wednesday of the year 1300, when Dante was 35 years old (midway through his three score and ten years). The journey takes roughly five and a half days. The year 1300 is significant other than being the midpoint of Dante's life. In 1300, spiritual repentance and spiritual renewal were major themes of the Catholic Church's first Holy Year.

• What is the scope of *The Divine Comedy*?

Herman Melville, author of *Moby Dick*, once said that in order to write a mighty book, an author needs to choose a mighty theme. By choosing the afterlife as his theme, Dante chose a mighty theme. He writes about the Inferno and how sins are punished, about Purgatory and how sins are purged, and about Paradise and how good souls are rewarded. In doing this, he writes about many themes that are important to people of his time and to people of our time and to people of any time: religion, God, poetry, politics, etc.

• **Is *The Divine Comedy* universal?**

"Universal" means applicable to anyone, at any time, and anywhere. Yes, *The Divine Comedy* is universal. One need not be a Christian to enjoy and learn from *The Divine Comedy*. All of us sin, and probably most of us regret sinning. Many people can identify with the characters of *The Divine Comedy*. For example, Francesca da Rimini refuses to take responsibility for her actions, instead casting blame on other people. Many of us have done exactly the same thing.

Reading *The Divine Comedy* seriously will take some work. Readers will need to know something about Dante's biography, about the history of his time and previous eras, and about literature. However, *The Divine Comedy* is relevant to our lives today, and this book and its companion volumes can be your guide to Dante's *Divine Comedy*.

• **What are some of the really big issues that are of concern to *The Divine Comedy*?**

One big issue is sin. For example, what are the results of sin?

One big issue is spiritual transformation. For example, how can one purge him- or herself of sin?

One big issue is politics. For example, Dante warns the reader about the dangers of extreme factionalism.

One big issue is poetry. How can poetry help us?

Of course, one really big issue is this: How do I enter Paradise?

• **This book can be your guide to *The Inferno*. What is the purpose of a guide?**

A guide will help you to cover territory safely the first time you go through the territory. However, many guides, including teachers, want to make themselves irrelevant. By reading this book as you read Dante's *Inferno*, you will get a good grasp of the material, but I hope that you continue to read *The Divine Comedy* and the *Inferno* on your own, making it a part of your life and going beyond what is written here. *The Divine Comedy* is one of the Great

Books of Western Literature — a book that you can reread with interest and profit each year of your life.

• **Briefly, what are the major facts of the biography of Dante the Poet?**

Dante was born in 1265 in Florence, Italy. He was successful in both poetry and politics. Early, he fell in love with Beatrice, a woman who died young in 1290. Both Dante and Beatrice married other people. About Beatrice Dante wrote a group of poems that he published in a volume (with commentary) titled *Vita Nuova* (*The New Life*).

Dante was a member of the political group known as the Guelfs, but when the Guelfs split into rival factions, he became a White Guelf. The White Guelfs opposed the Pope and wanted Florence to be free from papal power, while the Black Guelfs supported the Pope and were willing to do his bidding if he put them in power. Not surprisingly, Pope Boniface VIII supported the Black Guelfs, and he sent troops to Florence who took over the city in November of 1301. We can date Dante's exile from Florence at this time, but he was officially exiled in January of 1302. Dante never returned to Florence.

While in exile, Dante composed his masterpiece: *The Divine Comedy*. He died on Ravenna in 1321 at age 56.

By the way, "Guelf" is sometimes spelled "Guelph."

• **What does the title *The Divine Comedy* mean?**

Dante called his poem the *Commedia* or *Comedy*. In the 16th century, the word *Divina* or *Divine* was added to the title to show that it was a work rooted in religion.

The Divine Comedy is a "comedy" for two reasons:

1) *The Divine Comedy* was not written in Latin, but was instead written in the "vulgar" language of Italian. Being written in a "vulgar" language, the vernacular, it is written in a language that was regarded as not suited for tragedy.

2) The epic poem has a happy ending.

• **What is the difference between Dante the Pilgrim and Dante the Poet?**

Dante the Pilgrim is different from Dante the Poet. Dante the Pilgrim is a character in *The Divine Comedy*. At the beginning, he is naive and sometimes believes the spin that the sinners in the *Inferno* put on their own stories. However, Dante the Poet is an older, wiser Dante. Dante the Poet has journeyed throughout the Inferno, Purgatory, and Paradise, and he sees through the stories that the sinners tell in the *Inferno*.

Dante the Poet is the author of *The Divine Comedy*, whose major character is Dante the Pilgrim. Dante the Poet has more knowledge and experience than Dante the Pilgrim.

For example, Dante the Poet knows that he has been exiled from Florence because he is in exile when he writes *The Divine Comedy*. Because the poem is set in 1300, and Dante is not officially exiled until 1302, Dante the Pilgrim does not know at the beginning of the poem that he will be exiled. He will hear the prophecies of his upcoming exile that are made in the *Inferno*, but he will not fully understand that he will be exiled until his ancestor, Cacciaguida, clearly tells him that in the *Paradise*.

Dante the Poet is also more intelligent than Dante the Pilgrim. Dante the Pilgrim will sometimes be taken in by the spin that sinners in the *Inferno* put on their stories, but Dante the Poet knows that God does not make mistakes. If a sinner is in the Inferno, Dante the Poet knows that the sinner belongs there.

- **_The Divine Comedy_ is an allegory. Define "allegory."**

An allegory has a double meaning. It can be understood on a literal level, but also present is a symbolic level. Literally, Dante the Pilgrim travels through the Inferno, Purgatory, and Paradise. Symbolically, a human soul who will be saved faces trials, overcomes them, and achieves Paradise.

Allegories have many symbols.

- **What do you need to be in the Afterlife in Dante's Inferno?**

You must meet three criteria:

1) You must be dead.

2) You must be dead in 1300 (with a few exceptions where a soul is in the Inferno while a demon occupies the soul's body in the living world).

3) You must be a dead unrepentant sinner. (After all, if you were a dead repentant sinner, you would be found in either Purgatory or Paradise.)

- **What does it mean to repent?**

To repent your sins means to regret them. Of course, this does not mean regretting being caught for doing them, but regretting the sins themselves.

The sinners Dante will meet in the Inferno are unrepentant sinners. The repentant sinners he will meet in Purgatory treat Dante very much differently from the way the unrepentant sinners he meets in the Inferno treat him.

• **What is the geography of Hell? In *The Divine Comedy*, where is Hell located?**

Dante did not think that the world was flat. (Educated people of his time did not think the world was flat.) To get to the Inferno, you go down. The story is that Lucifer rebelled against God, was thrown from Paradise to the Earth, and landed on the point of the earth that is opposite to Jerusalem. His landing made the Southern Hemisphere composed of water as the land rushed under the water to hide from him. In addition, when he fell to the center of the Earth the land he displaced formed the Mountain of Purgatory.

Dante and Virgil will climb down to the center of the Earth, where Lucifer is punished, then they will keep climbing up to the other side of the world, where they will climb Mount Purgatory.

• **Explain the three separate kinds of moral failure: incontinence, violence, and fraud.**

Incontinence

Incontinence is not being able to control yourself. For example, you may not be able to control your sexual desire (lust) or your desire for food and drink (gluttony).

Violence

Violence can be directed against yourself (suicide), against God (blasphemy), or against other people (physical violence).

Fraud

Fraud involves the willful use of misrepresentation to deprive another person of his or her rights. For example, one can claim to be able to foretell the future and charge people money to tell them their "futures."

Simple fraud is fraud, but it is not committed against those to whom one has a special obligation of trust.

Complex fraud is fraud committed against those to whom one has a special obligation of trust. Sinners who commit complex fraud are traitors of various kinds: e.g., traitors to kin/family, traitors to government, traitors to guests, or traitors to God.

• **What kinds of characters will we see in *The Divine Comedy*?**

We will see both real characters and fictional characters. Mythological creatures will often be the guards in the Inferno.

Some of the characters will be important historically and globally, while others will be important only locally and would in fact be forgotten if they had not been mentioned in the *Inferno*.

• What do the sinners in the Inferno all have in common? Why can't we take what the sinners say at face value?

They have in common the fact that they are unrepentant. They do not take responsibility for the sins they have committed. Because of that, they will spin their stories and try to put the blame on someone or something else.

When we read the *Inferno*, we must be careful to try to see the whole story. The sinners will **not** tell the truth, the whole truth, and nothing but the truth. (Reading this retelling of Dante's *Inferno* or the notes in the translation of the *Inferno* that you are reading can help you to understand when a character is trying to spin you.)

Be aware that many people in the *Inferno* are going to be able to tell a good story, and you may end up thinking — like Dante the Pilgrim sometimes — that a certain sinner does not belong in Hell. However, Dante the Poet realizes that God doesn't make mistakes. Anyone who is in Hell deserves to be in Hell. It's important to closely examine the stories of some persuasive sinners to see what they are leaving out.

• Why do people sin?

Two main reasons, perhaps:

1) A lack of will. Often, we know what we ought to do, but we can't bring ourselves to do it. (Everyone who needs to lose 10 pounds knows exactly what to do to lose it: Exercise more and eat less. Someone who exercises less than they should and eats more than they should without a good reason such as illness is guilty of the sin of gluttony.)

2) An attractive veneer. Sometimes, sinning can appear to be attractive and to be fun, and thus people are tempted to sin. (Staying up late, getting drunk, and partying can be fun, but if these things prevent a student from attending class, that student is guilty of the sin of sloth.)

• Does God make mistakes? Do these sinners belong in the Inferno?

We must be careful when reading the *Inferno*. Dante the Pilgrim will sympathize with some sinners early in the *Inferno*, and we may be tempted to do exactly the same thing, but God is omniscient, omnipotent, and omnibenevolent. God does not make mistakes. If a sinner is in the Inferno, the sinner belongs there.

By the way, the difference between *Inferno* and Inferno is that *Inferno* is the title of a book and Inferno is the name of a place. (Similarly, *Hamlet* is the title of a play, and Hamlet is the name of a character in that play.)

Conclusion

Once you have read this retelling in prose of Dante's great epic poem *Paradise*, you will have a good but basic understanding of it.

Now go and read the real thing. I recommend the translation by Mark Musa. The translation by John Ciardi is also very good.

Appendix B: About the Author

It was a dark and stormy night. Suddenly a cry rang out, and on a hot summer night in 1954, Josephine, wife of Carl Bruce, gave birth to a boy — me. Unfortunately, this young married couple allowed Reuben Saturday, Josephine's brother, to name their first-born. Reuben, aka "The Joker," decided that Bruce was a nice name, so he decided to name me Bruce Bruce. I have gone by my middle name — David — ever since.

Being named Bruce David Bruce hasn't been all bad. Bank tellers remember me very quickly, so I don't often have to show an ID. It can be fun in charades, also. When I was a counselor as a teenager at Camp Echoing Hills in Warsaw, Ohio, a fellow counselor gave the signs for "sounds like" and "two words," then she pointed to a bruise on her leg twice. Bruise Bruise? Oh yeah, Bruce Bruce is the answer!

Uncle Reuben, by the way, gave me a haircut when I was in kindergarten. He cut my hair short and shaved a small bald spot on the back of my head. My mother wouldn't let me go to school until the bald spot grew out again.

Of all my brothers and sisters (six in all), I am the only transplant to Athens, Ohio. I was born in Newark, Ohio, and have lived all around Southeastern Ohio. However, I moved to Athens to go to Ohio University and have never left.

At Ohio U, I never could make up my mind whether to major in English or Philosophy, so I got a bachelor's degree with a double major in both areas, then I added a Master of Arts degree in English and a Master of Arts degree in Philosophy. Yes, I have my MAMA degree.

Currently, and for a long time to come (I eat fruits and veggies), I am spending my retirement writing books such as *Nadia Comaneci: Perfect 10*, *The Funniest People in Dance*, *Homer's* Iliad: *A Retelling in Prose*, and *William Shakespeare's* Othello: *A Retelling in Prose*.

By the way, my sister Brenda Kennedy writes romances such as *A New Beginning* and *Shattered Dreams*.

Appendix C: Some Books by David Bruce

Retellings of a Classic Work of Literature

Arden of Faversham: *A Retelling*

Ben Jonson's The Alchemist: *A Retelling*

Ben Jonson's The Arraignment, or Poetaster: *A Retelling*

Ben Jonson's Bartholomew Fair: *A Retelling*

Ben Jonson's The Case is Altered: *A Retelling*

Ben Jonson's Catiline's Conspiracy: *A Retelling*

Ben Jonson's The Devil is an Ass: *A Retelling*

Ben Jonson's Epicene: *A Retelling*

Ben Jonson's Every Man in His Humor: *A Retelling*

Ben Jonson's Every Man Out of His Humor: *A Retelling*

Ben Jonson's The Fountain of Self-Love, or Cynthia's Revels: *A Retelling*

Ben Jonson's The Magnetic Lady, or Humors Reconciled: *A Retelling*

Ben Jonson's The New Inn, or The Light Heart: *A Retelling*

Ben Jonson's Sejanus' Fall: *A Retelling*

Ben Jonson's The Staple of News: *A Retelling*

Ben Jonson's A Tale of a Tub: *A Retelling*

Ben Jonson's Volpone, or the Fox: *A Retelling*

Christopher Marlowe's Complete Plays: Retellings

Christopher Marlowe's Dido, Queen of Carthage: *A Retelling*

Christopher Marlowe's Doctor Faustus: *Retellings of the 1604 A-Text and of the 1616 B-Text*

Christopher Marlowe's Edward II: *A Retelling*

Christopher Marlowe's The Massacre at Paris: *A Retelling*

Christopher Marlowe's The Rich Jew of Malta: *A Retelling*

Christopher Marlowe's Tamburlaine, Parts 1 and 2: *Retellings*

Dante's Divine Comedy: *A Retelling in Prose*

Dante's Inferno: *A Retelling in Prose*

Dante's Purgatory: *A Retelling in Prose*

Dante's Paradise: *A Retelling in Prose*

The Famous Victories of Henry V: *A Retelling*

Mankind: *A Medieval Morality Play* (A Retelling)

Margaret Cavendish's The Unnatural Tragedy: *A Retelling*

The Merry Devil of Edmonton: *A Retelling*

The Summoning of Everyman: *A Medieval Morality Play* (A Retelling)

Robert Greene's Friar Bacon and Friar Bungay: *A Retelling*

The Taming of a Shrew: *A Retelling*

Tarlton's Jests: A Retelling

Thomas Middleton's A Chaste Maid in Cheapside: *A Retelling*

Thomas Middleton's Women Beware Women: *A Retelling*

Thomas Middleton and Thomas Dekker's The Roaring Girl: *A Retelling*

Thomas Middleton and William Rowley's The Changeling: *A Retelling*

The Trojan War and Its Aftermath: Four Ancient Epic Poems

Virgil's Aeneid: *A Retelling in Prose*

William Shakespeare's 5 Late Romances: Retellings in Prose

William Shakespeare's 10 Histories: Retellings in Prose

William Shakespeare's 11 Tragedies: Retellings in Prose

William Shakespeare's 12 Comedies: Retellings in Prose

William Shakespeare's 38 Plays: Retellings in Prose

William Shakespeare's 1 Henry IV, aka Henry IV, Part 1: *A Retelling in Prose*

William Shakespeare's 2 Henry IV, aka Henry IV, Part 2: *A Retelling in Prose*

William Shakespeare's 1 Henry VI, aka Henry VI, Part 1: *A Retelling in Prose*

William Shakespeare's 2 Henry VI, aka Henry VI, Part 2: *A Retelling in Prose*

William Shakespeare's 3 Henry VI, aka Henry VI, Part 3: *A Retelling in Prose*

William Shakespeare's All's Well that Ends Well: *A Retelling in Prose*

William Shakespeare's Antony and Cleopatra: *A Retelling in Prose*

William Shakespeare's As You Like It: *A Retelling in Prose*

William Shakespeare's The Comedy of Errors: *A Retelling in Prose*

William Shakespeare's Coriolanus: *A Retelling in Prose*

William Shakespeare's Cymbeline: *A Retelling in Prose*

William Shakespeare's Hamlet: *A Retelling in Prose*

William Shakespeare's Henry V: *A Retelling in Prose*

William Shakespeare's Henry VIII: *A Retelling in Prose*

William Shakespeare's Julius Caesar: *A Retelling in Prose*
William Shakespeare's King John: *A Retelling in Prose*
William Shakespeare's King Lear: *A Retelling in Prose*
William Shakespeare's Love's Labor's Lost: *A Retelling in Prose*
William Shakespeare's Macbeth: *A Retelling in Prose*
William Shakespeare's Measure for Measure: *A Retelling in Prose*
William Shakespeare's The Merchant of Venice: *A Retelling in Prose*
William Shakespeare's The Merry Wives of Windsor: *A Retelling in Prose*
William Shakespeare's A Midsummer Night's Dream: *A Retelling in Prose*
William Shakespeare's Much Ado About Nothing: *A Retelling in Prose*
William Shakespeare's Othello: *A Retelling in Prose*
William Shakespeare's Pericles, Prince of Tyre: *A Retelling in Prose*
William Shakespeare's Richard II: *A Retelling in Prose*
William Shakespeare's Richard III: *A Retelling in Prose*
William Shakespeare's Romeo and Juliet: *A Retelling in Prose*
William Shakespeare's The Taming of the Shrew: *A Retelling in Prose*
William Shakespeare's The Tempest: *A Retelling in Prose*
William Shakespeare's Timon of Athens: *A Retelling in Prose*
William Shakespeare's Titus Andronicus: *A Retelling in Prose*
William Shakespeare's Troilus and Cressida: *A Retelling in Prose*
William Shakespeare's Twelfth Night: *A Retelling in Prose*
William Shakespeare's The Two Gentlemen of Verona: *A Retelling in Prose*
William Shakespeare's The Two Noble Kinsmen: *A Retelling in Prose*
William Shakespeare's The Winter's Tale: *A Retelling in Prose*

Anecdote Books

250 Anecdotes About Opera
250 Anecdotes About Religion
250 Anecdotes About Religion: Volume 2
The Coolest People in Art: 250 Anecdotes
The Coolest People in Books: 250 Anecdotes
The Coolest People in Comedy: 250 Anecdotes
Don't Fear the Reaper: 250 Anecdotes
The Funniest People in Art: 250 Anecdotes
The Funniest People in Books: 250 Anecdotes
The Funniest People in Books, Volume 2: 250 Anecdotes

The Funniest People in Books, Volume 3: 250 Anecdotes

The Funniest People in Comedy: 250 Anecdotes

The Funniest People in Dance: 250 Anecdotes

The Funniest People in Families: 250 Anecdotes

The Funniest People in Families, Volume 2: 250 Anecdotes

The Funniest People in Families, Volume 3: 250 Anecdotes

The Funniest People in Families, Volume 4: 250 Anecdotes

The Funniest People in Families, Volume 5: 250 Anecdotes

The Funniest People in Families, Volume 6: 250 Anecdotes

The Funniest People in Movies: 250 Anecdotes

The Funniest People in Music: 250 Anecdotes

The Funniest People in Music, Volume 2: 250 Anecdotes

The Funniest People in Music, Volume 3: 250 Anecdotes

The Funniest People in Neighborhoods: 250 Anecdotes

The Funniest People in Relationships: 250 Anecdotes

The Funniest People in Sports: 250 Anecdotes

The Funniest People in Sports, Volume 2: 250 Anecdotes

The Funniest People in Television and Radio: 250 Anecdotes

The Funniest People in Theater: 250 Anecdotes

The Funniest People Who Live Life: 250 Anecdotes

The Funniest People Who Live Life, Volume 2: 250 Anecdotes

The Kindest People Who Do Good Deeds, Volume 1: 250 Anecdotes

The Kindest People Who Do Good Deeds, Volume 2: 250 Anecdotes

Maximum Cool: 250 Anecdotes

The Most Interesting People in Movies: 250 Anecdotes

The Most Interesting People in Politics and History: 250 Anecdotes

The Most Interesting People in Politics and History, Volume 2: 250 Anecdotes

The Most Interesting People in Politics and History, Volume 3: 250 Anecdotes

The Most Interesting People in Religion: 250 Anecdotes

The Most Interesting People in Sports: 250 Anecdotes

The Most Interesting People Who Live Life: 250 Anecdotes

The Most Interesting People Who Live Life, Volume 2: 250 Anecdotes

Resist Psychic Death: 250 Anecdotes

Seize the Day: 250 Anecdotes and Stories

Children's Biography

Appendix D: Some Books by Brenda Kennedy (My Sister)

The Forgotten Trilogy
>Book One: *Forgetting the Past*
>Book Two: *Living for Today*
>Book Three: *Seeking the Future*

The Learning to Live Trilogy
>Book One: *Learning to Live*
>Book Two: *Learning to Trust*
>Book Three: *Learning to Love*

The Starting Over Trilogy
>Book One: *A New Beginning*
>Book Two: *Saving Angel*
>Book Three: *Destined to Love*

The Freedom Trilogy
>Book One: *Shattered Dreams*
>Book Two: *Broken Lives*
>Book Three: *Mending Hearts*

The Fighting to Survive Trilogy
>Round One: *A Life Worth Fighting*
>Round Two: *Against the Odds*
>Round Three: *One Last Fight*

The Rose Farm Trilogy
>Book One: *Forever Country*
>Book Two: *Country Life*
>Book Three: *Country Love*

Books in the Seashell Island Stand-alone Series
>Book One: *Home on Seashell Island* (Free)
>Book Two: *Christmas on Seashell Island*
>Book Three: *Living on Seashell Island*
>Book Four: *Moving to Seashell Island*
>Book Five: *Returning to Seashell Island*

Books in the Pineapple Grove Cozy Murder Mystery Stand-alone Series

Book One: *Murder Behind the Coffeehouse*

Book Two: *Murder in the Library*

Books in the Montgomery Wine Stand-alone Series

Book One: *A Place to Call Home*

Book Two: *In Search of Happiness...* coming soon

Stand-alone books in the "Another Round of Laughter Series" written by Brenda and some of her siblings: Carla Evans, Martha Farmer, Rosa Jones, and David Bruce.

Cupcakes Are Not a Diet Food (Free)

Kids Are Not Always Angels

Aging Is Not for Sissies